VOLUM

THE
ADVENTURES
OF
RUSTY REDCOAT

By Ernest(Ernie)Gordon

With My Best Wishes

Ernie Gordon

Nov 2014

CONTENTS

FOREWORD

by Professor David J. Bellamy. OBE

My first contact with Red Squirrels was with Squirrel Nutkin in Beatrice Potter's book. This book was one of the first things to spark my interest in natural history, the beginning of my lifetime adventure. Growing up in Surrey, a lifetime ago, the countryside was rich in wildlife, hazel coppices, old woodland with Oak, Beech and Sweet Chestnut, perfect feeding grounds for the Red Squirrel. Sadly the Grey Squirrel came on the scene and things became less perfect. The Red Squirrel numbers dropped dramatically with only small 'pockets' of our indigenous creature now remaining in England.

Efforts to redress the balance in numbers are ongoing but, I was recently introduced to a little fellow by the name of Rusty Redcoat who is doing more than most to raise public awareness of the Red Squirrels' plight. Ernie Gordon, who dramatises Rusty's adventures, might well be the 21st century's answer to the Squirrel Nutkins of today.

A fascinating read with a big message.

REVIEW

A Review by Cameron Cochrane, aged 10.

 Having read my Grand Uncle Ernie's book about 'The Adventures of Rusty Redcoat', Volume One, I was thrilled to learn all about the amazing antics and wild ways of the young red squirrel, Rusty, who was rescued as a helpless infant by Sonny, the gamekeeper's son, when their tree house drey was tragically demolished in the woods near Alnwick in England.

Rusty really is an amazing character with a free, wild, spirit all of his own and nothing seems to stop him from achieving just about anything he sets his mind on to realise his dream and return to his family back in his original woodland home.

Now, Grand Uncle Ernie has completed **volume two** of Rusty's adventures and I am delighted to have been asked to review this second book, all about the perils Rusty faces, along with his brother Len, when out on the wild, rugged and dangerous moorland in his attempt to return home where, together, they face many dangerous challenges on the way when their very lives are, so often, at risk.

Each chapter is full of intrigue and daring in order for them to survive and be reunited once again with their beloved parents, Duke and Duchess Redcoat, sisters Milli and Yum. All of whom are known as the 'Millennium Family' !

While I was kept in suspense and a high state of excitement with each and every chapter, I am sure the reader, just like me, will be terribly saddened at the final outcome to learn just how the very existence of the Red Squirrels in England is seriously threatened and to allow such an evil, deadly, affliction to remain unchallenged for so long to the detriment of our own, beloved, British Red Squirrels is a terrible shame.

Nature will normally take care of it's own but, there are times when we humans have to be more active to help poor creatures such as 'Red Squirrels' in their time of need. **Scotland be warned**.

As the story unfolds, the reader will soon begin to understand the real purpose behind Grand Uncle Ernie's creation of the Rusty Redcoat adventures which you will really appreciate fully once you have read volume two from start to finish.

Junior Editor

RECAP OF VOLUME ONE

REMINDER

'Rusty escaping from captivity at the Croft as illustrated in Volume One'

The reader may recall, if they have read Volume One, just how Rusty Redcoat almost lost his life when the mechanical tree monster chopped down the tall pine tree in which the Redcoat family home was located and how his mother, Duchess Redcoat, had managed to rescue his two sisters and brother, Milli, Len and Yum, the 'Millenium' Family, just in time before the tree top drey crashed to the ground with Rusty Redcoat still inside.

Although knocked unconscious, Rusty was rescued by Sonny, son of the Gamekeeper Kevan, who just happened to be passing by, and Rusty was taken into captivity way up at The Croft on the side of Alnwick Moor where Sonny lived, away from all Rusty's family and woodland friends.

Despite being kept in a life of luxury with a wonderful cage, and the most delicious food, Rusty could not accept this strange way of life and waited for the day when the opportunity would arise to allow him to escape. That day finally came when he was able to free himself but not before he had caused a great deal of mayhem and damage inside Sonny's bedroom and elsewhere. He also had to defend himself against such evil enemies as Rotter Rat in the old barn, to which he had been banished by Sonny's father Kevan, as well as having to put up with the terrifying antics of Terry the family pet terrier dog.

It was during Rusty's attempt to return to his family, miles away in the woodlands near Alnwick, when, on several occasions, he had had to fight for his very life out in the wild countryside as he attempted the most hazardous journey of his young existence. Nor was he aware that his long lost brother Len, accompanied by their illustrious father Duke Redcoat, had left the wild woodlands in an attempt to rescue Rusty and that his father Duke had sustained very serious injuries as a direct result of an encounter with the evil, and ferocious, predator Buzz Buzzard.

Still far from his woodland home, Rusty was about to experience yet more hair raising adventures as he makes a valiant attempt to reach home alive and so, Volume Two will take you on this exciting journey where you will read about the many more wildlife adventures, surprises, delights and finally, bitter disappointment, all of which will be sampled throughout the twenty two chapters of this book.

Although based on a fictitious account of a Red Squirrel and his family, in particular, young Rusty Redcoat, the final outcome is, in reality, a true, sad, terrible and tragic situation which now prevails within the wild, and managed, woodlands in and around Alnwick, and throughout the Border Counties of Northumberland but, to a lesser extent in Cumberland.

In effect, the numbers of red squirrels have been so tragically reduced to a small percentage of those existing when 'The Adventures Of Rusty Redcoat', Volume One, was first published seven years ago as a direct result of the invasion of the alien, disease ridden, Grey Squirrel species in Northumberland which has, already, virtually annihilated almost the whole population of red squirrels throughout England and beyond, with a deadly plague which has raged unchecked these past fifty years. WHY?

Ernest (Ernie) Gordon

Author

Chapter One

OH' WHAT A DANGEROUS LIFE

Roxy Fox, a full cousin of Ray Reynard, was loping along in the shadow of the dry stone wall with his nose close to the ground, following the strong scent of a red squirrel and licking his lips in anticipation of a tasty breakfast.

The scent was fresh which Roxy had picked up further back at the point where Rusty Redcoat had spent the night inside the wall and Roxy knew that his breakfast was not too far ahead so he quickened his pace a little.

Up ahead, Rusty's mind was now focussed on food, not having eaten for several hours. He really wanted wholesome food to give him plenty energy for the journey ahead and also, he knew he would no longer be able to rely on Sonny to provide him with a regular supply of scrumptious cornflakes and *white water*.

Having covered quite a lot of ground alongside the moorland wall, Rusty knew he simply had to survey the land ahead before travelling any further and, with only a leap and a bound, was on top of the wall in a flash, surveying the open moor in the morning sunlight.

'Rusty taking his bearings and looking out for predators from the top of the old stone wall'

Some distance ahead, Rusty spotted a clump of trees and bushes situated about fifty metres to the east of the wall. This was not really a safe place to be but the little *hunger gremlin* inside Rusty's stomach was demanding to be fed and the temptation was too much to resist.

Keeping low and also in the shadow of the wall, Rusty travelled on until he was directly opposite the small copse and, once again, scaled the wall to check the area for any danger which may be lurking close at hand. With no obvious sign of danger, Rusty leapt from the top of the wall straight into a bed of reeds and sped as fast as he could in the direction of the clump of trees.

He was soon stopped dead in his tracks for, after only after a few metres, he was confronted with not one, but two of the most unusual creatures he had ever set eyes on and who, equally, were staring back at him, never having seen such a tiny red and white creature out on the wild moorland in their lives before..

Rusty eyed these two evil, black faced sheep, with curled horns protruding from either side of their heads, with the utmost intent and kept a good distance from them in case they chose to attack.

The more Rusty stared the less he became alarmed because there was a certain something about these weird creatures which did not send any signal of alarm to his brain but, nevertheless, he remained cautious before deciding which way to get past these two giants whose mouths munched continuously as they chewed sideways on nothing in particular.

Rusty could simply not understand this continuous chewing, 'After all' he thought, 'they are not really eating anything' !

These were none other than two members of the Black Faced Sheep flock who live out on the wild moorland all the year round yet, and quite unbeknown to the stray red squirrel, their very act of curiosity was sufficient to give away his position should any winged predator be looking on. 'Better to be safe than sorry' was Rusty's idea as he moved on in a wide arc so as not to upset the two *woolly weirdos.*

'Two craggy black faced sheep on the wild moor'

2

Rusty was having to dodge the large clumps of tough, tubular grass which made it difficult to keep in a straight line and furthermore, made it impossible to see where he was going at all. For such a small creature, the large clumps of reeds are similar to large, tall bushes to a human being by comparison and Rusty knew he had to check his direction repeatedly in case he became hopelessly lost.

As he moved forward to find another high point he stumbled out of the reeds onto a well worn sheep track and found himself staring at the tops of the trees he had seen earlier from his position on top of the wall. This is when all four of Rusty's legs went into *overdrive* as he sped like a rocket towards the trees as if his life depended on it, which it really did.

Little did he know that Roxy Fox had now reached the point when his nose told him his breakfast, or was it now lunch, had changed direction at right angles to the wall and was now heading straight for the copse which he knew very well indeed for this is where he often sheltered on a cold, wet night when he was out hunting on the moors.

Rusty meanwhile had finally reached the safety of the trees and was immediately seeking out the tallest tree to climb, way up off the ground to the highest possible twig. Once up there, he breathed a huge sigh of relief for Red squirrels are always at their most relaxed and comfortable when they are high up in the branches for this is the safest place to be for these skilful climbers.

From way up on the highest point of the old Ash tree, Rusty had a marvellous view of the entire countryside. Most of the moorland was now coloured in a light brown carpet of bracken and heather and the dry stone wall seemed to stretch for miles. Almost directly below Rusty could now see a great number of Black Faced sheep as they grazed nonchalantly among the heather but was unable to recognise the pair he had met earlier, they all seemed to look identical.

Suddenly, three or four of the Black Faced flock abruptly lifted their heads as if startled by something nearby. Then several of them turned sharply and ran quickly away, all in the same direction for about thirty metres, then all the flock in the immediate vicinity stopped grazing and did likewise. Rusty could now see about fifty or more black faces all turned and gazing in the same direction. 'What on earth could have caused these peaceful creatures to suddenly become alarmed'? Rusty thought to himself.

Following the direction of the startled sheep's gaze, Rusty easily detected a movement way down below, a movement which he immediately recognised. It was, as a very young red squirrel, when out one day away from the drey with his family in the woods for the very first time. He had been first to spot Ray Reynard, the famous old fox, when his mother, Duchess Redcoat, had given a timely alarm call which had brought Rusty, together with Milli, Yum and Len, his brother and sisters, scampering up from ground level to safety. Now, looking down from his lofty vantage point, Rusty soon detected the slinking movement of another fox. This was certainly not Ray Reynard because Rusty could clearly remember every marking on that evil creature which his sister Yum had, quite wrongly, believed was like a *giant red squirrel.* !

Rusty's sharp eyes were now focussed directly on the approaching *killer* as it trotted along the well worn sheep track towards the copse where Rusty believed he had been entirely safe from any predator. The sudden arrival of the terror fox caused Rusty, once again, to switch on all his alert signals in preparation for what might lie ahead. Despite the imminent danger, the little *hunger gremlin* inside Rusty's stomach was protesting strongly that no food had yet been received *down there* therefore, he decided to ignore the presence of his enemy for now as he was not in any immediate danger and went off in search of a well earned meal.

On his way in search of food up in the treetops Rusty had, quite unconsciously, memorised a convenient tree hole and also what appeared to be a discarded Magpie's nest. These locations he subconsciously stored away in his memory as his mind was totally focussed on food.

Rusty was soon feasting on the most tasty acorns. The nearby Oak tree was absolutely laden with fruit, more than enough to satisfy the *tiny gremlin* down below.

The feeling of being free at last, even though still a long way from his woodland home, made Rusty ever so happy and content, especially as he climbed about in the ancient Oak tree selecting only the ripest of fruit. Even a slight movement in the undergrowth below as Roxy Fox prowled about was not sufficient to cause Rusty any concern as he leapt from one branch to another with all the skill of an adult red squirrel, or so he thought !!!

Spying what appeared to be the juiciest of all acorns on another branch close by, Rusty took off into mid air as his powerful hind legs catapulted him across the gap to land on what seemed to be a perfectly safe branch to settle on. As he extended his front paws to grasp the branch Rusty realised, all too late, that this particular branch was rotten and would not bear the weight of his *flying* body.

The moment his front paws settled on the rotting branch, Rusty knew he was in BIG trouble. With a sharp crack the rotten branch broke and Rusty found himself sailing through the air, still holding onto the broken branch, as he cried in despair, "Oooooooh, Noooooo, Not again !!" as the memory of that terrible day when the woodsman had cut down their treetop home when just a young *kitten* flashed through his mind.

The air was whistling past Rusty's ears as he hurtled towards the ground below when, in a flash, he let go the broken branch and spread his body like a *sky diver*, star fashion, as he prepared himself to land on the ground.

Luck, once more, was on Rusty's side as he fell to ground. He managed to grab hold of a tall Willow sapling which bent double under his weight but, fortunately, reduced the severity of the impact as he hit the ground with a thud.

Fortunately for Rusty, he had managed to land on a soft bed of dried leaves and reed grass which the wind had previously blown into a mound to form a cushion for him to land on otherwise, he would surely have broken every bone in his body. Even so, his head was full, once again, of bright, shiny stars as he lay there in a daze.

Rusty knew in a fraction of a second that he was in desperate trouble but also realised he was not injured in any way. Still dazed, he struggled to recover his senses as he staggered to his feet when all around him seemed to be *misty*.

Very loud alarm bells were ringing in his head and a strange, distant, voice was calling to him "fox, fox, fox", as if to warn him of the danger he was in.

Roxy Fox had lost no time as he had heard the desperate cry from Rusty and had caught a brief glimpse of the red squirrel falling from a great height, still clinging to the broken branch. Seizing the opportunity, Roxy sped through the undergrowth, hoping to find a readymade *lunch* lying on the ground but was hampered by the dense bracken and brambles which covered the ground.

Meanwhile, Rusty had buried himself in the dry leaves so as to hide himself from view until his head stopped spinning. Slowly the fog in his head began to clear as he peeped out above the leaves and studied the situation.

Roxy was too anxious to get to the fallen red squirrel by the shortest possible route and soon found himself hopelessly entangled in the thorny brambles as he attempted to force an exit. Hundreds of needle sharp barbs tore lumps of fur from his body and many thorns penetrated his skin as he attempted to find a way through.

From the mound of leaves, Rusty soon became aware of Roxy Fox nearby, struggling in the undergrowth, and his sensitive nose told him that the strong smell it had detected was indeed that of a fox. Of that there was no doubt.

Without a second thought, Rusty leapt from the bed of leaves in a flash and reached the trunk of the old Oak tree in two seconds and climbed up to the first branch he came to. He perched himself safely to observe the ground below and at once became aware of the awful pains which seemed to be aching in every joint of his tiny body.

This, of course, was the after effects of having fallen from such a great height where only the willow branch had softened his fall sufficiently and which had undoubtedly saved his life. Quickly forgetting his aches and pains, Rusty soon spotted the frantic movement in the bramble patch below as Roxy Fox struggled to free himself.

Rusty also quickly realised just how lucky he had been to have escaped the jaws of this hungry fox for, had Roxy chosen to circle around the bramble patch instead of trying to force his way through, then most surely he would have sniffed him out in the pile of leaves and that would have been the end of Rusty Redcoat.

Roxy Fox finally freed himself from the painful trap he had created for himself because of his own carelessness and Rusty was beside himself with pride as he watched the bedraggled creature trail its *stinging* body around the bramble patch to squat at the foot of the tree.

To have been on red squirrel alert had, once again, helped Rusty escape certain death and humiliate the big dishevelled brute below who was now busy trying to extract some of the many bramble thorns which were painfully embedded in his skin. All to Rusty's sheer delight.

But Roxy Fox was not the only one who was in pain. As Rusty began to make his way further up the tree, he soon found out just how stiff and sore he was as all four limbs refused to react in the normal lightning fashion. The location of the old Magpie's nest, and the tree hole, were clear in Rusty's mind now, only he was unable to leap from branch to branch to make his way quickly to either of them as the bright sun rose to it's highest position of the day.

What with his ordeal of the past hour or so, and the heat of the sun, Rusty was dreadfully thirsty and tired. His stomach rumbled as usual for want of a drink but he must rest awhile to allow his aching body to recover.

As he sat observing his surroundings, and the miserable fox lying at the foot of the tree, Rusty glanced about him to see what his next move must be when he looked again at the old Magpie's nest and the tree hole at the same time. The hole in the tree appeared to be closest as he dragged his aching limbs along several branches and finally reached the hole. Not caring what, or who, maybe already inside, Rusty was only too pleased to gain access into the hole and sleep for a 'whole week' !

Within two minutes he was fully content, relaxed, and fast asleep but his automatic red squirrel alarm system did not switch off at all because it was trying to identify the continuous 'Bzzzzzzzz' sound which signalled danger and seemed to echo inside the tree hole, and ALL AROUND OUTSIDE !!

'Rusty exploring the hole in the old oak tree'

Chapter Two

BLACK AND YELLOW INVADERS

The shock of the fall had sent Rusty into a deep sleep the moment he lay down inside the hole up in the tree. The end of his bushy tail was sticking out just a little beyond the entrance and whatever it was he was dreaming about caused his tail to twitch now and then.

Under normal conditions, Rusty would have curled his tail over his back in typical red squirrel fashion but to-day, being so hot, was the exception. It was just as well really, because he was about to experience the most painful alarm call of his young life, even more painful than the bites on his nose end previously by Wally Weasel and Rotter Rat.

Even the 'Bzzzzzzz' sound earlier had failed to register in his brain as an alarm signal, such was the effect the terrible fall had had upon him.

Now, just after mid-day, the sun was at its hottest which was causing a great stir in a nearby dead tree trunk that housed an overcrowded hoard of black and yellow Wasps. Not only was the burning sun to blame but the added cause of commotion was a second Queen wasp was now present inside the heaving mass of crawling creatures occupying the nest and this was just too much for the thousands of angry occupants to tolerate. *Something had to give.*

The wasp's nest was so overcrowded that there was not sufficient space inside to allow cool air to flow, so the temperature inside became unbearable as did the temper of each individual wasp.

It was quite clear that two Queens could not occupy the same nest and one of them had to leave. It was the duty of several wasp *scouts* to go in search of another suitable nest hole and it was actually one of these searching *scout* wasps who had earlier discovered the hole in which Rusty was sleeping and which his red alert system had failed to recognise the buzzing of the wasp's wings as a sign of danger.

As the searching wasp returned to double check the hole again, it became entangled in the hair of Rusty's tail and, already being in a vile temper because of the situation in the old nest, became extremely angry indeed, especially when the sleeping owner of this bushy tail sensed the presence of some interfering creature and, unconsciously, flicked his tail to dislodge it.

Now there was *no* way this ill tempered wasp was going to accept this sort of treatment, especially when he had discovered a new home for his Queen, and the hairy occupant would have to be evicted by the only means he knew how.

Still struggling to escape from the *hairy* trap, the wasp injected the tip of Rusty's tail, not once but three times in succession, with a dose of poison so powerful, in fact, it almost rendered the sleeping Rusty Redcoat unconscious.

Rusty's dream suddenly became a nightmare as he felt his tail go completely numb. This feeling convinced the drowsy red squirrel that someone, or something, had cut off his tail and the pain in his rump was now unbearable as he struggled to shake off his drowsiness.

It took a great effort for Rusty to get to his feet as the burning feeling in his hindquarters felt as if he was on *fire*. It clearly was most unlucky for Rusty to have come in contact with an ill tempered wasp who was able to repeat his terrible sting over and over again. Had it been a garden, or wild, bee then Rusty would have received only one, less painful, sting but then sadly, the bee would have died a very painful death.

This is because nature has provided the bee with a hook, or barb, on the end of its sting which it cannot withdraw after use. It is for this very reason that the bee dies as a result of not being able remove the sting, which is so sad.

The wasp, on the other hand, can inject repeatedly because its sting is similar to that of a sharp pointed needle.

Fighting off the desire to lie down and sleep, Rusty realised that if only one wasp could cause him so much pain then a lot of wasps would kill him very quickly and so he struggled to regain his senses.

Meanwhile, the lone wasp, who had attacked Rusty, was buzzing its way back to the old rotting tree trunk, and the writhing hoard of angry wasps, to tell them that HE had discovered the ideal place to bring the new Queen wasp and many hundreds of her devoted followers.

In a matter of minutes, the air outside the old wasp's nest was alive with a mass of excited, buzzing, black and *yellow invaders* who had gathered in a great seething ball in mid air as they surrounded their new Queen. The lone scout wasp who had discovered the new nesting place, at present occupied by Rusty Redcoat, was getting ready to lead the flying multitude of worker wasps towards their new home in the tree, now creating a noise as loud as a vacuum cleaner and moving ever closer to Rusty's position.

Still suffering from the sleepy trauma brought about by the wasp's venom, Rusty was trying very hard to recover his senses and realised he was now in mortal danger. His whole body ached as he tried to turn around inside the hole and he desperately wanted to get out of there to safety as the *buzzing ball* of wild wasps was getting closer and closer.

From the outer edge of the hole he could now see the moving swarm about ten metres away but it was the searching soldier and worker wasps which alarmed him most who were much closer as they began to explore their new nest site from which Rusty was wanting to escape.

With his hind quarters still numb, Rusty was able to climb from the hole which was normally quite natural to him but, he had no feeling in his hind legs whatsoever. Instead he had to lower his aching body down the trunk of the tree using only his front paws. To have climbed further upwards would have meant certain death because the hundreds of excited soldier wasps would easily have detected his presence and quickly attacked and stung him to death.

'Rusty leaves the hole in tree as wasps take over'

11

Slowly, and in great pain, Rusty managed to move further and further away from the tree hole as he made his way down the tree trunk. Glancing upwards, he could plainly see the advance party of wasp soldiers checking out their new home to see if it was suitable for the new Queen and the buzzing of their wings echoed inside the hole louder than ever. Rusty was greatly relieved to see they were all too interested in their new home to be bothered about him as he neared ground level and possible safety.

Still suffering terribly from the poison *injected* by the wasp, Rusty was trying hard to keep his mind clear. He knew only too well that he may have escaped with his life up in the tree but now, almost on the ground, what, or who, could be lurking in ambush. His whole body was aching and all this was on top of the painful fall he had experienced earlier. His tail was burning hot where the wasp had stung him three times and he was in no fit state to be roaming around on the floor of the small woodland copse for too long, especially when Roxy Fox was on the prowl.

Rusty's tongue was dry as *old sticks* and, on top of all his other troubles, the little food *gremlin* was protesting angrily, yet again, that he had not had anything to eat for ages !

Upon reaching ground level, Rusty discovered a shallow ditch which provided good cover to get him well away from the angry swarm of deadly wasps, who were now attempting to enter the tree hole to get their precious Queen safely inside. Glancing up the tree once again, Rusty was relieved to have escaped certain death and his aching body shuddered at the thought of being trapped inside that hole with an army of soldier wasps about to attack him.

Moving on carefully down the line of the ditch, Rusty came upon a small pool of crystal clear water from which he drank gleefully to quench his thirst and also, to keep the little *hunger gremlin* quiet, at least for a little while longer. The long drink of ice cold water seemed to revive the lucky red squirrel and so, he turned around and, ever so slowly, lowered his *burning* tail down into the pool. The instant relief was so satisfying that Rusty decided to attempt something he had never, ever, in his young life, done before as he gradually moved backwards to submerge his whole body in the cold but soothing water.

Now this was a most unusual and dangerous thing for a red squirrel to attempt, especially as he was putting himself in a dangerous situation but it was a risk he simply had to take if he was to be able to move freely.

The sheer bliss of the *cold bath* seemed to remove all the aches and pains, as if by magic, and Rusty knew he would soon dry out in the warm afternoon sun.

The drink alone had revived Rusty sufficiently to call upon all his natural instincts of survival as he continued down the ditch towards another old nobbly Oak tree. From what Rusty could see on the ground was enough to tell him there was food a plenty about but he must climb up, way above ground level, to savour the delicious acorns yet, he could not resist picking up a lovely fat juicy one from the ground before he scampered up to the lowest branch with the acorn in his mouth. It was on the stout branch of the ancient Oak tree that Rusty spread himself full length to allow the sun to dry his wet, rusty coloured coat while he devoured the tasty acorn at the same time.

The flavour of such a delicious fruit was sufficient to silence the little *food gremlin* down inside but not enough to satisfy Rusty's appetite as he struggled to climb up to the higher braches because he still ached a little and thought to himself. "Whatever will I do if the wasp poison has caused permanent damage to my body" ? That awful thought was soon forgotten as he tucked in to more juicy acorns as the afternoon sun glistened on his beautiful shiny fur coat and soon his little white belly was quite full.

The old Oak tree was the tallest in the copse and from his position on the uppermost branch Rusty decided he must discover his exact whereabouts as he scanned the moorland around him but all was not as it should be.

As he attempted to look out across the moors all seemed hazy and unclear as he rubbed his eyes with his fore paws. For some reason, Rusty's vision was blurred because he could not even see the nearby dry stone wall clearly as he rubbed his eyes even harder.

Glancing at the ground below, Rusty suddenly realised that something was terribly wrong with his eyes because everything seemed strange as if he was looking into a mist. His mind had earlier been totally focussed on choosing the ripest acorns to satisfy his appetite that he failed to notice the problem with his eyesight and now he was instantly aware that the poison in his tiny body from the horrible wasp stings had finally affected his vision.

It was also time to find a resting place for the night as the sun sank ever closer towards the top of the moor to the west, that much Rusty could not fail to recognise when the little *gremlin* down below, never satisfied, again reminded him that a drink of water was urgently required !

Rusty's close-up vision seemed to be OK as he began to scale carefully down the tree trunk on his way to that little water hole he had used earlier in the day and he made it to ground level without any trouble at all. He back tracked his way along the shallow ditch and was soon gulping down the cool clear water as quick as he could swallow, ever mindful of any danger which may be lurking close at hand.

Instantly, every hair on his body stood on end as a slight sound up ahead caused him to prepare himself for an urgent escape. It could only have been the movement of a small twig on the ground, ever so slight, but there was no doubt in Rusty's mind that danger was present and he was thankful that the wasp poison had not affected his hearing.

The sound of dry leaves on the woodland floor was now distinctly louder and Rusty did not waste another second as he shot like a rocket away from the nearby prowler, pleasantly surprised that all his limbs now seemed to be working without too much pain. In about five seconds he found himself at the foot of a large pine tree as he leapt upwards to gain a firm foot hold with all eighteen sharp claws which helped him climb to immediate safety about ten metres above ground.

Puffing and panting to regain his breath following such a frantic dash, Rusty realised just how much the deadly wasp venom had affected his every movement as he recovered on the stump of a pine branch.

Even with his vision impaired, a sudden movement below prompted him to squint down with half closed eyes to detect the blurred picture of the panting Roxy Fox at the foot of the pine tree who, once again, had not been smart enough to out- wit the intelligent Rusty Redcoat, even though he was badly handicapped with the effects of the wild wasp's stings.

Now safe from the *giant* killer, Rusty could simply not resist the temptation to 'wee' all over Roxy Fox from his lofted position of advantage, ten metres above. This was the first time ever that Rusty had resorted to such a rude gesture which he had first seen used by adult red squirrels way back in his wooded homeland when he was just a tiny kitten and it gave him a great thrill to do so for all the fear and anxiety Roxy Fox had caused him in his attempt to turn Rusty into a tasty meal . Not at all happy at being 'weed' on from above, Roxy retreated to a safe distance and turned to look up at the tiny, disgusting, little creature with a threatening stare which seemed to send a clear message to Rusty of "Just you wait mate, I'll get you for 'weeing' all over me" !!

Sticking out his chest with pride at having humiliated Roxy Fox, Rusty skipped up through the pine branches to explore the top of the tall tree and for once that terrible day, luck was on his side.

Almost at the very top, Rusty discovered a discarded nest, only a flat bed of twigs and dry bracken but ideal for him to rest upon in the dense foliage.

He was soon curled up on his temporary bed and, even though the sun was not about to set for at least another two hours, he settled down for a well earned sleep. Despite all his aches and pains, plus the fuzzy vision in his eyes, Rusty relaxed at last .The only sound he could hear, oddly enough, was that of the buzzing worker wasps as they flew backwards and forwards, to and from their new nesting place, loaded with pollen to feed the huge wasp family in the tree hole. They were no longer interested in the rusty red ball of *fluff* who, only about three hours ago, were just about to kill him to take over the tree hole as a nesting place.

Sleep finally came to the little adventurer. No need to wrap his tail around himself as the hot sun of the day had warmed the air that he was soon in his own land of dreams as the large old pine tree swayed ever so gently in the evening breeze.

Chapter Three

RUMOURS GALORE

Up at The Croft on Alnwick Moor, Sonny was beside himself with sorrow at the loss of his tiny pet red squirrel, Rusty Redcoat, as was his Dad Kevan. No one seemed to know just who had been neglectful in leaving the window open or how Rusty had managed to release the catch on the cage door or, had that been left open as well ?

Sonny had not eaten at all for two whole days, such was his sadness, despite the damage Rusty had caused in his bedroom and he knew in his heart that a search of the surrounding moorland would prove to be a waste of time because he believed Rusty was now back in the forest with his family and woodland friends.

Nor did Sonny realise just how close his father Kevan had come to finding Rusty the morning after his escape when he set off a booming blast from his shotgun as he had passed directly below Rusty who lay hidden in a hole up in the old tree.

Even though Sonny accepted the fact that he had lost his furry friend, he strongly believed that, at sometime in the future, he would meet up with Rusty Redcoat once again. Of that he had no doubt.

Way up north at the *wildlife café* on the edge of the forest, where Isobel and Oliver provided the finest food for miles around, the rumours and gossip were all about the missing Duke Redcoat and his son Len who had set out to rescue Rusty a few days ago and had not been seen since.

There was no way that Duchess Redcoat, Rusty's mother, could fail to learn about the stories of her husband and son Len and she became most distraught and saddened at all these negative tales. It was her two daughters, Milli and Yum, who comforted her by insisting that the whole family would all be reunited in the very near future, for that is what they most firmly believed.

Despite his terrible injuries after the battle with Buzz Buzzard, Duke Redcoat had made a marvellous recovery as he lay deep inside the old rabbit warren. His wounds had healed very well because he had been able to bathe them twice daily at the little moorland stream close by and now he felt strong enough to return to the woods and allow his son Len to continue in his attempt to rescue Rusty from captivity.

'The rabbit warren where Duke Redcoat took refuge after being injured by Buzz Buzzard'

Duke knew he could return to the woods without any fear of embarrassment at not having rescued his son Rusty because the visible scars on his body were sufficient proof that he had been lucky not to have lost his life in the skirmish with Buzz Buzzard. The ugly wounds were there for all to see and would remain visible until his fur grew back again.

Len, meanwhile, had left the safety of the deserted rabbit hole early that morning and plotted his course from the low sun in the east which would lead him in the direction of the old dry stone wall but first he had to travel some distance over open moorland which, at this time in the morning, was full of hungry predators searching for breakfast.

All along the track, Len's sensitive nose was identifying scents and smells of previous users who had travelled along its winding course during the night. Most prominent, and obnoxious, was the pungent smell of Nadger Badger and his gang but Len could also identify the positive traces of a wandering Fox, a slinking Stoat and those of the moorland sheep who had created this path in the first instance many, many generations ago.

As he loped along at a steady pace, Len's mind was focussed on his plan, a plan he had devised earlier in the safety of the discarded Rabbit hole, of a way to get to The Croft, the home of gamekeeper Kevan and his son Sonny where, he believed, his brother Rusty was still being held in captivity. Of course, Len was not to know that Rusty had since escaped and was, in fact, less than one mile distance from him at that very moment.

Hunger, as usual, was also prominent in Len's mind as he approached a solitary old and craggy Oak tree situated alongside the track which many hill sheep used to shade them from the hot sun in summer time. Directly below the tree was hard packed, bare, soil and Len soon spotted several acorns lying around, sufficient to satisfy his appetite for the time being.

Just as soon as he had devoured a hearty breakfast, Len leapt onto the old stunted trunk and scrambled up to the topmost twigs which gave him a marvellous vantage point from which to scan the countryside around him as the sun rose steadily in the clear, blue morning sky.

Quickly, Len took stock of his surroundings and the scene ahead then carefully lowered himself to a more secure position with a stout branch behind his body as a precaution against any flying predator who may, already, have spotted his presence.

Due south of his present position, Len made a mental note of the start of the dry stone wall which his now badly injured father Duke had told him about. This wall threaded itself along the side of Alnwick Moor for a great distance and, as Len traced its line in a south westerly direction, he could just make out a faint shape of several stone buildings which he knew to be those of The Croft and his heart sank as he quickly realised just how far he still had to travel to arrive at his destination.

Len was not in the least encouraged as he studied the landscape ahead because the expanse of moorland was totally barren, with only the occasional tree for cover on his desperate journey. There was however, a cluster of tall trees about a mile ahead, to the left of the wall, which Len made a mental note, just in case he should need to make his escape in an emergency. Little did he know that in this copse were two very active and angry wasp's nests, a very sly and determined fox and his long lost brother Rusty, still fast asleep on a discarded Wood Pigeon's nest.

All of a sudden, Len was very scared indeed. Not having been away from the safety of his woodland home before, the familiar smells his nose detected on the moorland track frightened him because there were not many safe trees immediately around him by which he could easily escape should danger arise.

Also, he no longer had his father, Duke Redcoat, for company and this unfamiliar landscape seemed to be full of dangerous predators, at least, according to his nose !. Nevertheless, he must reach the dry stone wall before nightfall if he was to be safe and sound. Once he reached the wall he would be able to plan the next stage of his rescue mission.

No sooner had Len climbed down to ground level to continue on his journey when, with a completely silent approach, 'Ken' Kestrel, another of the Hawk family, swooped over the dried bracken and *lighted* on the topmost twig of the old oak tree which Len had vacated, minutes before.

'Ken' Kestrel very quickly spotted the bobbing tail belonging to Len as he bounced along the pathway. To 'Ken', this bobbing tail had the sign *breakfast* written all over it as he took off from the top of the tree to stalk his prey.

Now the Kestrel is a very fussy hunter because he, or his partner 'Kate', always like to study their potential victim carefully before diving in to attack. They are so easy to recognise as they hover in mid air, just like a *feathered helicopter*, for several seconds, even a minute or two, before diving down for the kill and this is precisely what 'Ken' Kestrel did as he took up his position above the unsuspecting red squirrel in the clear morning sky.

Two things happened simultaneously. One, 'Ken' folded his wings as he began his dive, hoping to take the running red squirrel from behind as he sped like *'greased lightening'* to capture his breakfast.

Secondly, the shadow of a passing Pigeon flashed across the track as it passed between the sun and the running red squirrel, just in front of the nervous Len Redcoat. This sudden, darkened, movement so startled the already frightened red squirrel that he took a headlong dive, quick as a flash, into the dense, dried bracken on the side of the track just a fraction of a second before 'Ken' Kestrel swooped by with extended talons, only to snatch at fresh air.

Len was not even aware of just how close he had come to death as he scampered deeper into the dense carpet of light brown bracken then lay flat in the undergrowth, not allowing a single hair on his whole body to move.

This ploy Len knew only too well from his woodland training for, when perched up in a tree, he could easily detect the movement of any woodland creature below simply because moving foliage gave away their position.

'Ken' Kestrel also knew this trick as he took up a new position in mid air, thinking that the wily red squirrel had *eyes in the back of its head* ! He could not recall when last he had missed such an easy target as this and really believed that the clever *wee red* had outwitted him.

From his position above, 'Ken' Kestrel again hovered silently and menacingly, looking for the slightest movement of foliage below but what he did not know was that 'Len' Redcoat had a clear sight of the fluttering Hawk as he lay motionless beneath the dense carpet of bracken, not even daring to tremble with fear !

This challenge of patience only ended when 'Ken' Kestrel convinced himself that the little red squirrel had been smart enough to escape his clutches as he swept away to search another area of wild moorland for a possible breakfast.

Len lay for ages below his *blanket* of bracken, totally unaware of just how close he had come to a fight for his very life because he was almost as big as Ken Kestrel who would not have been able to lift Len off the ground. The wounds he would have sustained from the Kestrel's talons would have rendered him helpless and unable to defend himself and he really was one very lucky young red squirrel.

Now positive that danger had passed, Len stirred carefully and stretched his body full length to relax all his joints which had become cramped after lying rigid for so long and now he was ready to resume his journey. Peeking out from the edge of the track all seemed clear as Len checked every point of view up and down the moorland pathway before continuing south on his way to find the beginning of the dry stone wall.

Anxious to check his position once again, Len spotted a small Rowan tree, otherwise known as the Mountain Ash, about ten yards up on the high side of the pathway and he had to crawl through the dense bracken to reach the tree which was laden with bright red berries. Even though Len was desperate for some food, his woodland experience told him not to touch these Rowan berries as they were terribly bitter and strictly not on any red squirrel's *menu*.

Len knew that the Blackbird and Thrush, and certain other birds, would only attempt to eat these berries as a last resort as they contained a high level of acid, most difficult to digest and not very tasty.

From this high view point, Len was able to plot the next stage of his journey and, without delay, found his way back to the pathway and moved on at high speed towards the dry stone wall from where he would decide just what the next stage of his plan would be.

Even though the sun was now at its highest point of the day, Len's nose was still able to detect the strong scent of other travellers who had used this trail but these were not fresh smells and Len knew he could safely travel on, knowing that the path ahead was clear of *trouble*.

Or was it? Suddenly he found himself on a double track and the bracken was no longer there. Instead, Len was now out in open grassland which was the feeding ground for a great many black faced sheep, each with curled horns, which made them appear very menacing indeed.

This was not the case however, but Len was not to know that these hill sheep were so placid, and timid, they simply carried on eating grass and took not the slightest notice of the tiny red squirrel as he stared guardedly at all the ragged, woolly creatures on the hillside.

To leave the cover of bracken behind made Len rather nervous knowing that he had no protection whatsoever as he worked out in his head just which way to travel. He was at a disadvantage being so small, and at ground level, that he had to rely on the sun to point him in the right direction which would eventually bring him to the dry stone wall. Len's concentration was rudely disturbed by the strange noise of some mechanical *thing* rapidly closing in on him up the double track and he was forced to dash back into a small patch of bracken behind him not knowing exactly what to expect as the mechanical *thing* roared closer and closer.

Len first observed the cloud of swirling dust as he peeked his head out from the bracken on the side of the track and the roar of the machine was almost deafening. Within seconds, it thundered by, driven by a *masked* rider wearing a strange hat and accompanied by a black and white Collie Dog who was getting an uncomfortable ride in the wire cage mounted on the back of the machine.

"What a strange sight" thought Len as he drew back to avoid the choking cloud of dust but he was not to know that this was the hill Shepherd who tended all the black faced sheep on the wide expanse of moorland and his faithful sheepdog called Spot. No doubt because he had a prominent white spot in the centre of his black forehead !

Once the dust had settled, Len set off at great speed along the double track with the thought of danger ever present in his mind because he had no protection at all out in the open and his shiny, rusty coat would easily be spotted by any winged predator who just might be in the vicinity.

Up ahead, another single sheep path led off the double track and Len knew instinctively that this was the path to take. Once on this trail, his nose soon detected a number of strong smells which told him who had travelled this way earlier in the day when, after about ten minutes of travelling at full speed, a large stone pillar loomed up before him which signified the beginning of the long, dry stone wall.

With a feeling of relief, and pride, Len was happy to climb to the top of the stone pillar to study the landscape ahead and could just make out, way in the distance, shapes of the buildings which he knew again, must be those of The Croft where he believed his brother Rusty was being *held captive*.

Taking a long drink of cool moorland water, Len proceeded to journey alongside the wall where he felt much happier and secure to be away from the open grassland. His nose was now working overtime as he travelled because of the increased number of *tell-tale* smells and his mind was now on food and also, where he was going to spend the night as the sun was dropping sharply over the west side of the moor.

As Len journeyed alongside the wall his nose began to quiver and the whiskers on either side of his nose trembled with excitement because one smell in particular, however faint, brought him to an abrupt halt, for this was indeed a scent which had Len shaking with glee. His nose quivered at the scent he had detected, the scent of none other than his beloved brother Rusty. Of that he had no doubt.

With intense concentration, Len trailed his sensitive nose close to the ground so not to lose the smell but, the excitement was almost too much for him to bear as he trailed slowly along in the shadow of the wall yet, all the while, keeping a watchful eye open for any possible danger which may be lurking nearby.

"Surely this cannot be" exclaimed Len to himself as the still faint scent of his brother Rusty continued as Len followed the unmistakeable trail. Even though other animals had passed this way, there was no mistaking the positive identification of Rusty and Len now knew he had to stop and gather his excitable thoughts together.

What Len had failed to recognise was that the light had suddenly become much gloomier in the past half hour and, as his stomach, again, rumbled in protest through lack of food, Len now decided that it was far more important to find somewhere safe to spend the night and so, with another strong unpleasant scent of the dreaded Weasel in his nose, he found himself looking up at a convenient hole in the wall which called for further investigation.   Climbing inside, Len was almost overcome with the powerful scent of his brother Rusty and he now knew, without any doubt whatsoever, that he would not have to travel on to The Croft to find his brother because Rusty Redcoat was very close at hand !

Chapter Four

ALMOST THE GREAT RE-UNION

Rusty Redcoat lay ever so still on the bed of twigs, which had been the nest of a Wood Pigeon, and every joint in his tiny body, from the tip of his nose to the tip of his tail, ached as a result of his dreadful fall from the top of the tree yesterday plus, the lethal attack from the menacing wasp, because his tail was still rather numb and tender.

He had spent a most uncomfortable night on the bed of twigs, especially as one particular twig, right in the middle of the old nest, was protruding upwards and sticking painfully into his side which he could not avoid, no matter how much he tried. As he stretched his limbs, as was his custom each morning early, Rusty believed he would never be able to run and climb again, such was the soreness and stiffness of his whole body and, as sleep began to clear from his fuzzy head, all the crazy events of the previous day became apparent to him.

Furthermore, even in his dreamy state of mind, Rusty realised just how stupid he had been to choose this old Wood Pigeon's nest as a resting place and knew perfectly well that he was the luckiest red squirrel on the planet to have survived the night, unprotected, out in the open.

The tiny *hunger gremlin* in his stomach was too weak for want of food to cry out in protest and the pangs of thirst and need of food were even worse than the aches and pains he was suffering in the rest of his body as he studied his surroundings in the early morning light. First of all, he had to leave the old nest of twigs immediately for his own safety, knowing that dawn was the most dangerous time of any day because *breakfast hunters*, of all descriptions, were now out and about on the prowl for whatever they could find to eat.

The effect of the wasp sting poison had left Rusty with blurred vision, even after so many hours, and he was going to need all his skill and attention this very morning if he was to avoid more danger. As if by instinct, Rusty managed to climb to the topmost branches in order to make clear in his mind his immediate surroundings when, even with his blurred vision, he quickly noticed a small shiny reflection which he instantly recognised as a pool of water and breathed a sigh of relief. He knew that as long as he could take a drink of water then he would survive to find solid food later on as he carefully worked his way down to ground level with every nerve strained to detect any hint of danger.

The delight of that early morning drink filled Rusty with an eagerness and vigour he thought he'd lost as he crossed the floor of the small copse to reach the base of the ancient Oak tree where he knew there would be an abundance of acorns.

There was only one snag, and it was a very big and dangerous snag, he had to get past the hole in the ancient Oak tree, yes, the very same hole which now housed a thousand or more wild wasps and which had been his refuge two nights ago !

The speed at which Rusty collected his thoughts and made his plan was nothing like the speed by which he climbed up the trunk of the ancient Oak tree. He sped past the entrance to the wasp's new home in a flash yet did not detect any sign of activity. Maybe wasps are not early risers like red squirrels but Rusty was relieved, nevertheless, to have reached the outer twigs where he knew the most delicious acorns would be.

He was not disappointed and was soon *tucking* in to a typical autumn breakfast and, as he ate, it seemed as if all his aches and pains, yes, and even his blurred vision, had left him and he began to feel as if, at last, he was back to his normal active and energetic self again.

A cloudless morning sky gave Rusty a clear view of the surrounding countryside as he scanned the panorama around him while he ate breakfast. Even as he ate, Rusty's sharp eyes detected every movement in the sky, as well as at ground level, but it was a movement on the ground nearby on which he now focussed his attention.

A disturbance in the undergrowth caused a small sapling to shake as the moving body of the prowler below had pushed it to one side and this movement gave Rusty all the information he needed as he stiffened, still as a statue, watching the stealthy creature whom he recognised instantly as no one other than Roxy Fox, where the white tip of his trailing tail was like a waving flag to the observant red squirrel.

Up in the Oak tree, Rusty knew he was not completely trapped because there were other trees close by to give him a means of escape however, the crafty Roxy Fox had not entirely recognised this fact.

From his lofted position, Rusty knew this was going to be another waiting game as he studied the situation on the ground below. The drink of water and his breakfast of acorns had fortified the lone red squirrel and prepared him for the long vigil which was just beginning because, once again, it was his very life at stake and one silly mistake could well be the last mistake he would ever make, such was the position in which he now found himself.

Not only was he at risk from the enemy below but, especially at this time in the morning, he was also a target for any flying predator and he, quite naturally, moved down to position himself below a stout branch, safe from the roving eyes of the enemy above.

It would have been a simple matter to move on but for some mysterious reason, Rusty decided to stay put.

At just about the same time that Rusty had woken up on his bed of old twigs, Len Redcoat stirred inside the dry stone wall and, just like his brother Rusty who, earlier, had felt the emptiness inside his stomach plus a terrible thirst for want of a drink.

Len had used the wedge of stone, exactly as his brother had done, to act as a door to protect him through the long dark night and this he now carefully removed and peered cautiously out to survey his position. The faint sound of water trickling nearby told Len that, at least, he would soon be able to quench his thirst but not before he had checked thoroughly that all was safe to do so.

'The long dry-stone wall where Len Redcoat finally spots his brother Rusty'

27

Refreshed by the long cool drink of moorland water, Len ventured up to the top of the wall to scan the countryside around him when, to his complete surprise, he noticed the clump of tall trees over to the east, the very same copse he had spotted from the top of the Rowan tree yesterday. Len could hardly believe he had travelled so far and, for some very strange reason, which as yet he could not quite understand, he suddenly became extremely interested in these trees which, even at this early hour of the day, seemed to shimmer in the bright, early morning sunlight as he took up a better position in order to study the scene before him.

Rusty, on the other hand, had a much higher vantage point up in the ancient Oak tree as he scanned the open moor land over in the west. With the morning sun on his back, Rusty had no problem seeing every detail with his extremely good eyesight, which had now fully recovered, as he could clearly see the dry stone wall where he had encountered the terrifying Wally Weasel and his gang a few days ago.

In a fraction of a second, the slightest movement way, way over on the dry stone wall had every hair on Rusty's body standing on end in total surprise and excitement. With a trembling body, which almost caused him to loose his balance, the image he had just seen was, undoubtedly, that of another red squirrel, of that Rusty Redcoat was absolutely sure. No doubt whatsoever.

For the very first time since that tragic day in the woods, where he had narrowly escaped death when the mechanical tree monster had felled the tree in which Rusty had been trapped, he began to quickly wag his bushy tail sideways. For this is the natural signal of all red squirrels everywhere as a sign of recognition, or a friendly greeting, to another red squirrel whenever they come in contact with one another.

Len, on the other hand, felt hypnotised as he stared into the bright shimmering haze of the early morning sun which caused him to squint through closed eyelids to avoid the glare. It was as if his heart missed a few beats when he detected the slightest movement in the large Oak tree which likewise, and in an instant, he too recognised as being the *tail signal* of another red squirrel.

Only the sixth sense of two red squirrels, especially two *blood brother* red squirrels, knew precisely that the signals each had seen, even from a long way off, was undoubtedly red squirrel language and two little hearts, even half a mile apart, pounded faster than a Woodpecker's courting call.

Simultaneously, Rusty and his long lost brother Len realised that they had finally found each other and also, each one knew that they would have to be bold, and very clever, if they were to safely negotiate that five hundred yard gap between them which they both knew to be full of numerous hazards but none more threatening than that of the dreaded Roxy Fox.

Roxy was not about to forget that it was the same little furry creature up in the old Oak tree who had wee'd down on him earlier and, for that very reason, was determined to seek revenge in the most terrible way possible and that was to capture and kill the impudent red squirrel if it was the last thing he ever did !

Roxy firmly believed he had the distinct advantage of being at ground level with a clear view of Rusty Redcoat up above in the Oak tree from which the red squirrel would have to climb down sometime because he could not stay up there forever and Roxy was prepared to wait all day if necessary as he licked his lips at the thought of a very tasty meal later in the day.

Now a Fox is just about the slyest, craftiest and deadliest of all woodland creatures and the most feared killer by far and Roxy was all of these, at least he thought he was ! As Roxy lay concealed in the undergrowth below he believed he had not been spotted by the red squirrel from above as he lay stretched out in a relaxed mood. So relaxed in fact that he was not aware that his bushy tail was slowly wagging backwards and forwards in contentment and that the white tip of his tail was clearly visible to Rusty Redcoat who was sitting on a stout branch above.

Rusty could only grin to himself as he watched the wagging tail below which was, to him, just like a *white flag blowing in the wind*. "You may think you are smart Roxy Fox" Rusty declared to himself, "but you are not as clever as one tiny red squirrel, and now *there are two of us*."!

Excited beyond belief, Len was anxious to reach his long lost brother without delay but was smart enough to carefully plot his journey between the dry stone wall and the small copse before making his move. He memorised the route he believed to be the safest and best before jumping down from the wall and headed towards the early morning sun with every hair on his body bristling with happiness as he skipped along to meet Rusty.

Rusty on the other hand was keeping a *canny eye* on the tiny moving speck in the distance and knew he had to devise a clever plan to out-wit Roxy Fox and this would have to include the safety of his long lost brother Len.

As he watched his brother travelling towards him, Rusty immediately began to send a warning signal with his tail which Len would soon recognise as he got closer and, all the while, keeping a watchful eye on the dozing Roxy Fox whose white tipped tail continued to wag in anticipation !

Len, meanwhile, had reached a *wispy* Elder bush which gave him an elevated view of the route ahead as he climbed the slender branch to plot the next stage of his journey. With his *x-ray* eyes focussed on the Oak tree ahead he immediately recognised the danger signal being sent by Rusty before the slender branch on which he was perched began bend down towards the ground under his weight.. But Len had received the warning tail signal perfectly clearly and *switched on* every sensitive whisker to red alert as he headed on eastwards towards his brother Rusty.

Roxy Fox now decided to move closer to the base of the large Oak tree just in case his *quarry* decided to make a dash to freedom and, once again, he settled down to wait in ambush. This movement was soon spotted by the observant Rusty who was absolutely delighted at this latest ploy by the fox as he squeaked in delight when the idea of his means of escape was immediately formed in his mind .

The nearest tree to the ancient Oak was a giant Scots Pine but it would require a gigantic leap to allow Rusty Redcoat to escape as the narrowest gap between the branches was two yards or more.

Rusty again tail signalled Len to make for the tall pine tree and watched eagerly to see if his brother had read his signal correctly. He did not have to wait too long before he saw the rusty *blur* of Len as he streaked across the open ground and scaled the lofty pine tree trunk at an amazing speed which left Rusty full of admiration at the way Len moved.

There was no further need for tail signals any longer as the two red coated brothers entered into a continuous *babble* of excitable *squirrel chatter* from one to the other which very soon became noticed by Roxy Fox. After all, it was many months since the two brothers were separated and neither could refrain from trying to tell the other as much as possible without stopping for breath !

At last the chatter ceased as Rusty told Len of his bold, but extremely dangerous, plan to escape the clutches of Roxy Fox and that he would not be able to do so without his brother's help and so the conversation continued in a more controlled fashion but, the best of all this was that, Roxy Fox could not understand a single word that passed between the two Redcoat brothers.

Len now took up a suitable position in the tall Scots Pine where he could clearly see the wagging white tip of Roxy's tail while Rusty went in search of a long, spindly twig by which he hoped to cause havoc down below in the undergrowth to enable his escape from the hungry fox and, only then, would he be able to greet his long lost brother Len with the biggest hug he had ever given in his whole life .

This is the tall Scots Pine Tree where the two Redcoat brothers were about to celebrate their re-union.

Chapter Five

A STROKE OF GENIUS

The mid morning sun told Rusty Redcoat that time was quickly moving on and that he must act soon if he was going to *out fox* Roxy Fox and escape with his long lost brother Len and seek a safe place to shelter during the night ahead. First of all he had to search the old Oak tree for a long slender twig with which to carry out his daring plan and was examining every branch on the tree until he spotted the ideal tool with which to arm himself.

It did not take him long to chew off the long twig, just as a Beaver would have done, by using his razor sharp teeth to gnaw through the base of the twig which he carefully dragged down through the thick branches and secured in the fork of one particular branch nearer to the ground.

In the tall Scots pine opposite, Len lay along one of the topmost branches watching his brother with curious interest, trying hard to understand just what he was up to as did Roxy Fox, down below, puzzled as to what the little red squirrel was playing at.

Rusty now passed on his instructions to Len in a deliberate form of squirrel *chatter* to which his brother instantly obeyed by positioning himself on a large pine branch which was heavily laden with huge pine cones, being the fruit of the Scots pine tree, as well as being a delicious meal for any red squirrel for the seeds it contains. Situated almost directly above the prone figure of Roxy Fox, Len was satisfied that all was in order as he silently sent Rusty a tail swishing signal that all was to plan and Len awaited instructions to *open fire* !

About two metres directly below Rusty's position on the main trunk of the ancient Oak tree was the wasp's nest which, by now, was a *hive* of activity as the many worker wasps were travelling to and fro, fetching and carrying pollen and nectar to build up their food store for the coming winter. At the entrance to the nest, being the hole in the side of the tree trunk, about forty or so soldier wasps were busy reducing the hole size by forming a barrier of chewed wax and tree bark to create a solid wall leaving only a small entrance, sufficient for only a single wasp at a time to pass through.

It was these soldier wasps who interested Rusty most and he studied their every movement intently knowing that two or three of them would kill him if they chose to attack. He carefully measured the distance between himself and the industrious soldier wasps and calculated in his mind just exactly how close he would be able to get without attracting their attention as he gingerly lowered himself into his final position and firmly grasped the end of the long slender twig.

Len went into action the very second Rusty gave the tail signal when he began to *bombard* Roxy Fox below with the huge pine cones. One after the other he hurled them down on the surprised creature with uncanny accuracy as the target below crawled closer to the trunk of the ancient Oak tree for protection from above.

At the precise moment, Rusty guided the end of the long slender twig slowly towards the entrance to the wasp's nest where, one by one, the soldier wasps gave up their building operation to attack the *strange stick invader*. Each soldier wasp attached itself to the end of the twig exactly as Rusty had anticipated and he could clearly see them repeatedly attempting to sting the *invader*. More and more soldier wasps joined in the attack until the end of the long twig held a writhing ball of angry, frantic, soldier wasps intent on *stinging the twig to death* !

At this precise point, Rusty carefully lifted the spindly twig containing the writhing mass of frantic soldier wasps and skilfully directed it over the bemused Roxy Fox below then, gently released his grip.

Roxy was otherwise engaged trying to dodge the barrage of heavy pine cones being directed at him from above by the excited Len Redcoat that he thought he was simply seeing double. "How come two red squirrels all of a sudden?" was the question which flashed through his mind as a long slender twig fell from above and landed across his back.

The sudden impact was sufficient to dislodge the ball of angry soldier wasps as the twig fell across Roxy's back, the shock of which caused him to move quickly away to seek cover. This movement proved to be Roxy's undoing as the *platoon* of soldier wasps launched their attack on the *giant hairy brute* as each wasp in turn buried itself in the shaggy fur of the fleeing fox and began to sting the unfortunate creature with their lethal stinging action, very much like the needle of a *sewing machine* !.

Never before had either Rusty, Len, or anyone else for that matter, ever heard a fox scream in terror as the dozens of lethal wasp injections penetrated his skin. Roxy's only action was to make for the dense patch of brambles where he proceeded to drag his whole body through the barbed entanglement to dislodge the stinging *black and yellow raiders*. Roxy's screams of pain must have been heard for miles around as he writhed and wriggled his way through the bramble patch from which he emerged almost numb with pain from the soldier wasp inflicted wounds and he bolted for the nearest ditch .

Roxy was soon stretched out, full length, in the bottom of the waterlogged ditch having got rid of the stinging horde and, oh, how he hurt from the tip of his nose to the end of his tail, his whole body seemed as if it was on fire.

Rusty meanwhile was almost mesmerised as he clung, rather transfixed, on the side of the tree trunk, unable to fully understand the pandemonium he had caused. He had simply wanted to distract the attention of the hungry fox, enough to escape from the tree to join his long lost brother Len and was totally amazed, and shocked, at the result of his actions.

Rusty really was troubled at the amount of pain he had caused Roxy Fox by way of his rather ingenious ploy and it was only the shrill chatter and warning calls from Len which brought him quickly to his senses.

In the tall conifer tree opposite, Len was absolutely thrilled at the part he had played in helping distract Roxy Fox by bombarding him with pine cones. He was also amazed by the ingenious way Rusty had sent Roxy Fox screaming through the undergrowth with a dozen or so angry soldier wasps attached to his shaggy coat.

"Wait 'til I tell Duke all about this, he will be so proud of us" thought Len when he suddenly noticed his brother was not to be seen in the old Oak tree. Rusty had wasted no time once Roxy Fox had run terrified from the foot of the old Oak tree. He leapt to ground once he had safely passed the entrance to the wasp's nest and streaked over the fallen leaves at breakneck speed to reach the base of the tall Scots Pine. The incredible speed with which he climbed up the enormous trunk had to be seen to be believed and, within seconds, he was perched on the uppermost bough where he was greeted by his beloved brother Len with a display of acrobatics, the like he had never seen before. The brotherly hug had said it all.

Rusty's tail was wagging like a *windscreen wiper in a rain storm* with excitement as he watched his brother perform the most incredible deeds on the end of the branch. Double, and even treble, somersaults were all included in his performance and he even raced round and round the branch as if attached to a piece of string, such was the skill and agility with which he greeted his long lost brother.

It took Rusty a while to calm his brother Len and, not wanting to spoil the re-union, approached him with an instant request and that was to get Len to chew off the confounded leather collar which had been a great source of annoyance since Sonny had fastened it around his neck all those months ago.

Instantly, Len set about the task with determination and chewed through the tough leather band in less than a minute. With immense relief, and pleasure, Rusty engaged in a thorough good scratch around his neck where the leather collar had almost removed the red hair beneath his chin while Len gleefully threw the chewed collar way down to the ground below.

The removal of the collar was cause for more acts of celebration as the two carefree brothers skipped and leapt with joy, just as they did on that very first day on the floor of the forest after leaving their woodland nest for the very first time.

The chatter was incessant as the pair of excited red squirrels began to relay their own stories of events which had happened since Rusty disappeared from their woodland home a long time ago and, as each had so many tales to tell the other, it would take weeks to complete !

At last the nose rubbing and brotherly slaps and playful antics stopped as each realised they should be making their escape while Roxy Fox was otherwise engaged soothing his painful body. Instantly, as is just about every red squirrel movement, they bolted down to ground level at breakneck speed and soon picked up the well worn sheep track which led them in a westerly direction towards the long dry stone wall and the wild expanse of windswept, barren moorland.

At the edge of the copse, the two brothers discovered some delicious sweet chestnuts lying amongst the leaves and immediately gathered a good quantity and quickly carried them up into a hollow in the nearby Sweet Chestnut tree, sufficient to fill the bellies of the two hungry red squirrels as they stuffed themselves full, knowing that this food could well have to last them until they finally reached their ultimate destination in the woodlands, yet so far away.

Both Rusty and Len found it almost impossible to concentrate on food as each one wanted to *blether* about so many things which had happened since they were separated many months ago, so excited were they at finding each other again after such a long time. Both had so many tales to tell but this would have to wait, at least for a few hours yet.

They agreed that it was necessary to reach the dry stone wall without too much delay. This would be the first stage of their long journey home, a journey which, no doubt, would be full of the unexpected and each young red squirrel would have to be on constant alert if they were to meet up with their loved ones and friends in the woodlands once again.

Rusty decided that this happy event was just too important to ignore as each brother had so much to talk about that he made up his mind to find a safe place to rest up following their tasty meal of sweet chestnuts. They would only stop for a drink of water as they made their way towards the dry stone wall for Rusty had already formulated his plan for the remainder of that day.

This was to use the tiny *cave* inside the wall, which had sheltered both of them, separately, in recent nights because it was now too late to embark on the long and dangerous journey home to the woodlands. Len disagreed because he wanted to move on to meet up with their father, Duke Redcoat, whom, he believed, would be anxiously awaiting them in the rabbit hole way up on the side of the moor where he was recovering from the terrible injuries he had sustained at the hands of Buzz Buzzard.

Len soon accepted Rusty's reasoning and so, after enjoying a long cool drink of water, they set off at a fast pace and were soon perched on top of an old tree stump, happy and content to be together again. The tales of past events were exchanged with great excitement as the two brothers chattered incessantly to each other, all the while keeping a careful lookout in case of danger.

Both had identified the smells of a good number of unfriendly visitors who had passed by recently such as Weasel, Stoat, Badger and even a dog of some description but, the strongest scent of all was that of the black faced sheep who regularly used this path alongside the wall when travelling to and from the little drinking hole but this smell did not disguise one smell above all others and that was the now very familiar odour of Roxy Fox or, at least, one of his close relatives.

Len found it hard to believe many of the strange tales Rusty told him simply because he had not experienced being in the captivity of a human family and found it difficult to understand their peculiar lifestyle.

Len in turn informed Rusty all about their father and mother, Duke and Duchess Redcoat, and explained just how much their two sisters, Milli and Yum, had now grown into two beautiful young red squirrel *ladies*, much sought after by other red squirrel males in the forest..

Rusty found it difficult to find words in red squirrel language to describe the mystery box in Kevan's bedroom which contained many tiny humans and he knew that, even if Len believed him, many of his woodland friends would not. Most of all, Rusty's chest swelled with pride as he told

Len about his daring deeds and how he had fought off two attacks from *Rotter Rat* and just how he had defended himself against, and outwitted, Wally Weasel and his large gang in the very same hole in the wall, which was only a few yards away, as they gabbled away incessantly to each other.

It was when Len imparted the news of the terrible injuries their father Duke had received from the razor sharp talons of Buzz Buzzard, while on their way to rescue Rusty, that the brave and fearless red squirrel was immediately overcome with grief at the thought of his famous and well respected father, Duke Redcoat, who was perhaps dying in that rabbit hole up on the moor. This sad news caused Rusty a great deal of inner pain, so much so, that their exciting stories immediately ceased as they began to form a plan to seek out their father at first light the very next morning.

Once again, the position of the sun in the west told both Rusty and Len that only a couple of hours remained for them on that day to prepare their lodgings for the night. They immediately began to gather mouthfuls of dried grass and bracken, sufficient to form a cosy bed inside the hole in the wall. With the stone wedge in place to keep out the most tenacious of raiders, both were entirely satisfied with their preparations as they settled down to a well earned, early nights' sleep but, not before more wonderful tales were exchanged until both very weary young red squirrels drifted off into a welcome, blissful, but not altogether, dreamless sleep.

'Rusty checking the hole inside the old dry stone wall'

Chapter Six

MEANWHILE, BACK IN THE FOREST

Unbeknown to the two intrepid Redcoat brothers, their father Duke had made a remarkable recovery from his injuries as he lay hidden in the abandoned rabbit hole up on the edge of Alnwick Moor. He had even gained sufficient strength to make the return journey back to the forest, which took him three long and painful days, where he was able to relay the news of his unfortunate experience to his wife Duchess and his two beautiful young daughters Milli and Yum who, together, immediately began to treat his terrible wounds as only wild female red squirrel *nurses* know how.

Duke reassured his wife and daughters that, as far as he knew, no harm had come to Len in his quest to find Rusty for surely, had anything out of the ordinary occurred then the moorland and woodland *grapevine* would have learned all about it and so far, *no news was good news.*

It was now the duty of the three females in the family to show their worth by lavishing all the gentle care and attention on the proud and noble Duke Redcoat as he lay-up in an old *drey* on the edge of a large *stand* of conifers. There was only one problem for Duke as he was being pampered and that was the continuous stream of questions which were being put to him by the three females who, quite naturally, wanted to know every minute detail about his rescue mission.

Unbeknown to the two daughters and her husband Duke, Duchess Redcoat was making regular trips over to the woodland *Café* situated on the edge of the forest where Isobel and Oliver, the kind and considerate humans, provided a constant supply of tasty tit-bits every day for all the visiting woodland creatures and, where she knew the slightest bit of news about her two *lost* sons would be talked about, for this is the headquarters where all the local woodland wildlife creature *gossip* is received.

On about her third visit to this wonderful *feeding station*, Duchess soon overheard a whisper that two red squirrels had been spotted in the isolated copse, way over on Alnwick Moor, by two sharp eyed crows as they flew overhead. They obviously had noted every detail of their sighting because there was mention of great excitement taking place in a very large Scots Pine tree which they had clearly seen from above as the two tiny red creatures were definitely celebrating some special occasion or happening.

This news, Duchess gathered, was about two days old but she was hardly able to contain her dignified manner as the excitement caused her to tremble all over, the way any loving mother would upon hearing such glad tidings. So, as not to falsely lift the spirits of Milli and Yum at this early stage, Duchess was careful to impart this wonderful news to her husband Duke only in the absence of their two daughters, at least for the time being.

Duke's return to the forest had been the most painful three days of his long and illustrious life as head of the proud and noble Redcoat family. He knew that unless he got back to his own familiar territory he would not survive much longer, especially if Wally Weasel and his ferocious gang should happen to pass by, for they would show not an ounce of mercy towards him and this is what drove him on.

It was this frightening thought which persuaded Duke to return to the forest where he would be able to recover from his injuries and leave the search for his lost son Rusty to Len.

As Duke lay dozing and resting his tired body, his thoughts returned to the nightmare journey which he had endured on his return to his home territory.

He had been so terribly weak, having lost such a lot of blood, he could only travel very slowly over short distances. He kept to the well beaten sheep paths which made travelling easier but this of course had exposed his presence to any flying predator passing overhead. Every so often he had to rest beneath the bracken and heather to recover and his mind was constantly on full alert which gave him a headache, especially when he was moving directly into the early morning sunlight, because the glare of the sun was like fire in his eyes.

On his first night out on the open moor, Duke was forced to build a bed of dry bracken and take the risk of being discovered but, it was a risk he had to take.

All seemed well until just before sunrise when Duke was disturbed from his deep sleep by the faint sound, and movement, of a creature close by as it attempted to gain entry into his hideaway. Right in front of Duke's nose the bracken was being forced inwards and suddenly the head of 'Sneaky Snout' Grass-Snake appeared with a darting tongue flicking backwards and forwards in an attempt to locate the occupant.

In one flashing movement, Duke let fly with his front right paw and the extended claws raked across the head of the invading reptile who withdrew his wounded head in an instant and slithered off into the bracken beyond to leave a very shaken Duke Redcoat shivering with shock knowing just how close he had come to being bitten by the lethal reptile. Had 'Sneaky Snout' Grass-Snake managed to sink his deadly fangs into Duke's body then the deadly poison would have entered his blood stream and slowly rendered the mighty Duke Redcoat paralysed. Duke knew he had been extremely lucky to survive the attempt on his life by the deadly snake and no wonder he was trembling like a jelly at the thought of what might have been.

But, there was absolutely nothing so frightening in the long life of the proud and noble Duke Redcoat as the dreadful sound of the low flying *mechanical monster bird* which caught him by surprise during his homeward journey.

This evil, mechanical, flying giant of the skies produced an horrendous, deafening, roar which Duke had heard on previous occasions but never so close as on that particular morning when the thunderous brute roared its way over the open moorland at a frightening speed. It caused the very air to vibrate and tremble as if the clouds would break into pieces and the ground beneath Duke's feet shook as if disturbed by an earthquake, such was the trail of absolute havoc left in the wake of this fearful and *hideous flying beast of the sky*. "What on earth would any human being want by creating such an abominable, peace destroying, evil, flying monster?" was the thought which was prominent in Duke's mind once he had recovered from the deafening ordeal which took him all of ten minutes to adjust to a normal level of hearing.

No living creature in the vicinity of this monster beast could escape the hideous blast of noise it produced and this included Duke's two adventurous sons, Rusty and Len, and Duke firmly believed it was the end of the world as the frightful *demon* screeched overhead on its way to *nowhere*.

At last, back in the old woodland drey, Duke was extremely grateful for the rest and treatment he was receiving from Duchess, Milli and Yum which was vitally necessary if he was going to re-establish his seniority as head of the red squirrel colony in the woodlands around Alnwick. He also knew that even though his cousin, Big Bob Blacktail, now back in Scotland, would try to return and take over the Redcoat leadership if anything should happen to Duke. For this very reason, Duke was determined to regain his strength and prove to every red squirrel in the land that he was still the Boss !

Meanwhile, over on the wide, wild, expanse of moorland, the two startled Redcoat brothers, Rusty and Len, were still recovering from temporary deafness after the horrendous blast from the flying brute overhead, fearing the very wall on which they were perched was going to collapse due to the unbelievable noise the aeroplane produced.

So engrossed had they been with each other's stories, they ignored the approach of the flying monster until it was too late. When they did recover their hearing, it was Rusty who was quick to point out to his brother that they must not be so careless in future or else they would definitely not make it safely back to their beloved woodlands if they continued to be so careless.

And so it was decided to take a last drink of water before they both gathered mouthfuls of dry grass and prepared their bedding for the night ahead in their *stone fortress* inside the wall. The entrance was barricaded against any likely intruder and the two tired brothers still found sufficient energy to chatter incessantly to each other for ages about things which had happened since the day when Rusty had disappeared.

Finally, tiredness overcame them when they curled up, cosy and warm, as they journeyed deep into dreamland, each by his own particular road.

Chapter Seven

WATER, WATER, EVERYWHERE

Inside the dry stone wall was about to become very wet indeed.

The two Redcoat brothers talked to each other for what seemed to be hours before they finally succumbed to sleep. Each with so much to tell the other about what had happened since they were separated on that terrible day when their treetop home was destroyed by the evil *mechanical tree monster*.

Despite their hectic activities during the long daylight hours, sleep was furthest from the minds of Rusty and his brother Len as they each, in turn, told tale after tale. Their excitement at meeting up again earlier in the day had not abated in the slightest and even the cold of the night had failed to penetrate their tired bodies until at last, as they snuggled down in the dry grass and moss, which they had gathered earlier for bedding, did they quickly realise that, in their haste to seek safety inside the wall, they had not gathered sufficient dry material to keep themselves comfortably warm.

Once the chatter finally ceased the two brothers tried in vain to relax their minds and bodies but the night wind outside on the wild moor grew stronger by the hour as it whistled through the gaps between the stones.

Sleep became impossible as the temperature inside their stone fortress dropped lower and lower, enough to cause the two tired red squirrels to shiver terribly with cold. Rusty used up almost all his bedding in an attempt to seal the gaps in the stonework which helped a little to keep out the cold draught but he knew perfectly well that if they were to survive the night, out in the bitter cold, then some drastic action was going to have to be considered.

Len was now in danger of being seriously affected by the alarming drop in temperature as he had never before experienced such terrible conditions. Life in the wild woodland was dangerous but one thing the Redcoat family were especially good at was to provide many safe, warm, dreys up in the tall pine trees, or else in some tree hole or other, simply because every minute of daylight is played out at such a frantic pace that, as darkness falls, all red squirrels virtually collapse with fatigue into the warmth and comfort of their luxurious night time accommodation.

Two of the prime requirements of any red squirrel are food and a warm comfortable bed and, at this particular time in the middle of the night, neither Rusty nor Len had either.

During his days in captivity, Rusty had certainly experienced the cold of the night, especially in the old barn but, what was about to happen next was totally new to the smart thinking Rusty Redcoat although brother Len knew all about the problems of RAIN.

Outside, the wind seemed to have dropped slightly, enough for two pairs of sensitive ears to hear the sound of heavy raindrops as they splashed down on the stones above. Soon a fine trickle of water found it's way into their *bedroom*, first from one direction then another, and it became very obvious to the two Redcoat brothers that the situation was now extremely serious.

Water began to pour into their little *stone lodgings* at such a rate as the deluge above continued, heavier than ever before, that, as if by telepathy, both scrambled at once to remove the stone wedge barricade from the entrance as the possibility of drowning became very real indeed.

Together they quickly pulled the stone wedge to one side but were unable to squeeze themselves out as both became trapped in the narrow opening in their haste to escape. Finally they managed to tumble outside in the pouring rain and into the pitch blackness of the night.

The ancient dry stone wall, once again, became their only form of navigation as they made their way in the driving rain to *dear knows where*. Neither had any idea which direction they were travelling because the pounding raindrops bombarded them with such force they could only squint through narrowed eyelids to keep the wall in sight. But, painful as it may be with the constant barrage of stinging balls of water, both realised that they had a much better chance of survival out in the open than they had trapped inside the wall.

At times, rivulets of water threatened to wash them away but now their eyes had become accustomed to the dismal gloom they were able to avoid the worst conditions and they plodded on regardless. Len trailed behind his brother for a while but then, suddenly, became insistent that he take the lead.

By reason of the dreadful conditions it was almost impossible to communicate with each other because their concentration was totally focussed on survival. Contact was made by way of touch and a series of high pitched squeaks which only a red squirrel could possibly understand. Rusty allowed his bedraggled brother to take the lead without protest because he recognised that Len had a positive plan as they climbed up the steep slope in the frightful rain storm.

A little way back down the track, Len had spotted a familiar land mark in the form of an old gate post, close to the wall. Through the darkness as the rain on the post reflected, ever so slightly, a signal of recognition in Len's brain, he knew he had seen before on his journey to find his long lost brother and a clear picture of the scene appeared in his head, just as clear as any playback system on a D.V.D, and he quickened his pace up the steep track.

Rusty immediately recognised the urgency in his brother's pace and eagerly followed close behind. The scene which Len now played out in his mind was of a strange structure which he had seen earlier in the week of a ramshackled shelter of corrugated tin sheets fixed crudely to the dry stone wall and the outer framework.

Len was not to know that this rickety building was in fact a shelter for the hill sheep in extreme weather conditions, such as those prevailing at present, and also, as a *maternity clinic* for the pregnant 'yows' (ewes) to give birth to their lambs in early springtime when snow lay on the ground.

Nevertheless, the two intrepid brothers journeyed on, becoming badly bruised and battered by the continuous onslaught of driving wind and rain. Their tiny bodies were now beginning to feel the effects of the violent storm as they struggled on but, Rusty was encouraged by the confidence he had in his brother Len.

Len was now clearly struggling up front against the howling wind and driving rain when Rusty decided to take over the lead. Even in the atrocious conditions he knew they must keep close to the wall as Len had assured Rusty that shelter from the storm was not too far away.

The two bedraggled and forlorn red squirrels now found themselves in conditions completely alien to them, or to any other red squirrel for that matter, and Rusty was now aware that the cold, and the rain, was beginning to have a serious effect on his brother who was becoming unable to keep up with Rusty's pace and thus causing him a great deal of anguish. The need to find shelter was now a matter of life or death.

A blurred image in the gloom ahead made Rusty pause, giving Len a chance to catch up and, upon hearing a squeal of delight from Rusty, he knew that, at last, the rustic shelter was now in sight.

Rusty suddenly bounded forward towards the blurred image of the hillside shelter for he could clearly hear the rain as it pounded on the corrugated tin roof. Despite the fatigue they were both suffering, Rusty took one almighty leap forward into the darkened gloom of the shelter, closely followed by a now excitable Len, to find themselves suddenly out of the horrible wind and rain, unable to see anything in the darkness but mightily relieved to be under cover at long last.

In the gloom, Rusty made his way forward with Len close behind when, to their absolute surprise and delight, they found themselves climbing up a great pile of wool which, to the two soaking wet and sodden creatures, was absolute bliss as they reached the top of the *woolly mound*.

Squeaks and squeals of sheer delight were abruptly halted as the *mound* of wool suddenly erupted upwards in the darkness and shook so violently, the two terrified brothers were forced to cling to the wool to avoid being flung out into the perils of the night as the large, and very angry, hill sheep jumped up and down trying desperately to dislodge the two *invisible raiders* who had chosen to *attack* her in the middle of the night and, in the middle of her dreamless sleep.

So violent were the antics of the startled sheep that both Rusty and Len were forced to leap to safety for fear of being crushed against the corrugated tin ceiling directly above their heads.

As if by telepathy, the two terrified red squirrels leapt out into the darkness together fearing the worst of all landings when, to their utter amazement, both ended up on a mound of dry, warm straw where they instantly tunnelled deep down inside to escape the wrath of the very angry hill sheep.

Together they continued to roll and frolic about to dry themselves in the luxurious straw and, despite more startled movements in the straw below from an equally startled family of field mice, the two extremely tired and bedraggled Redcoat brothers were soon in a deep, deep sleep without a care in the whole world, as was the old hill sheep.

The thunderous noise of the rain, still pounding on the corrugated tin roof outside, did not penetrate deep down in the straw where the two sleeping red squirrel brothers lay, oblivious to any sound whatsoever. Such was their fatigue as a result of their nightmare journey in the pouring rain and black darkness where they were almost 'unconscious' to anything going on around them. So deep was their sleep they were completely unaware of the disturbance taking place at the entrance to the shelter where, once again, the old hill sheep had her sleep disrupted, only this time the culprit was a great deal larger than the previous intruders.

The Reynard Fox family boasted a large number of adult members who roamed the countryside, mostly at night, in search of food to satisfy their insatiable hunger but, this particular *lady* member of the *Reynard Clan*, being a Vixen, was the mother of four hungry cubs and the atrocious weather did not deter her in the least as she scoured the countryside in search of a meal.

On previous occasions she had always managed to catch a few mice, or even couple of slinking rats, inside the old sheep shelter and she could almost have travelled there blindfold, such was her knowledge of that particular hillside, even in the pouring rain.

Vicky, for that was her name, Vicky Vixen Reynard to be exact, had fully expected to raid the old sheep shelter without any trouble but, as she moved forward towards the open end of the shelter she found her way barred by a very large and angry hill sheep, angry at having her *beauty sleep* disturbed twice in such a short space of time and determined that the wily mother fox was not going to cause havoc in her *bedroom*. NO WAY !!

No matter how she tried to gain entrance, Vicky was outsmarted at her every move by the determined '*yow*' who, with her horned head bowed low ready to charge the mother fox, for her head was her only means of attack. Vicky knew only too well that, even in the darkness, the powerful sheep could inflict terrible injuries upon her, especially if she was struck by one, or both, of her deadly horns which protruded from each side of her head.

Vicky Reynard knew only too well that, as the mother of four young cubs, she could not afford to challenge the angry sheep which, with the strong scent of a red squirrel in her nose, she was extremely disappointed but then she thought, 'What would a red squirrel be doing so far away from any woodland?' and made a mental note in her very astute 'brain box' because this was worth following up later on as she trotted away in the darkness of the appallingly wet night.

Both Rusty and his brother Len were not the only *red creatures* who occupied the rickety old shelter. Deep down below the straw an army of these tiny *rusty red creatures* were just about to begin a meal at the expense of the two Redcoat brothers who were in an almost *unconscious* sleep following their ordeal out on the wild, wet moorland.

The rain had now, thankfully, stopped as the first rays of early morning light began to illuminate the barren hillside as strange things began to happen beneath the cosy straw *blanket.*

Rusty and Len were not to know just how fortunate they had been earlier in the night when the old 'yow', who was now busy nibbling at the already new green shoots of grass as she grazed among the heather. For it was she who had warded off the hungry Vicky Vixen Reynard and undoubtedly saved the lives of the two sleeping red squirrels who were now beginning to stir beneath the straw. This was in fact a severe disruption to their beauty sleep as the first of the tiny red FLEAS descended on them in the straw and moved quickly into the fur of the now very warm and dried out red squirrel brothers.

At first Rusty believed he was being pricked by a sharp piece of straw and he quickly changed his position as did Len. More pricks were felt as the numbers of invading Fleas increased, biting through the skin of the two half asleep red squirrels as the Fleas sucked out their breakfast of BLOOD !

Suddenly the two sleepy headed red squirrels realised they were indeed being attacked by these *marauding blood sucking* creatures as they began to scratch frantically at every part of the body they could reach. At the same time they had to fight their way up through the huge mound of straw in an attempt to escape the biting pests who were now firmly lodged in the fur of the two rusty haired victims, in great numbers.

Even though roused from a deep sleep, Len at once recognised the tiny mites as blood sucking fleas but Rusty had not. He was writhing and leaping about like some demented soul when he heard the distinct call from his brother to follow him immediately as the two *flea ridden* brothers bolted from the hillside shelter as if fired from a *gamekeeper's gun.*

Even as they fled the shelter, the army of *minute blood suckers* were all clinging to the hair of their victims as they continued to devour their *blood breakfast* but Len knew instinctively just what he was searching for as he led his brother Rusty, at breakneck speed, along the muddy sheep path.

The torrential rain through the night was to provide the two tormented brothers with the very thing they had tried to avoid only a matter of a few hours ago when Len took a sudden twist in mid air to leap into a torrent of running water as it cascaded over a large boulder to form an almost perfect *shower* which poured down from the hillside.

In a fraction of a second later, Rusty was alongside Len as they stood below the stream of ice cold water combing their soaking hair with fingers and toes, using their long claws to seek out the *ferocious tiny invaders* and wash them away in the pouring stream down into the heather and bracken from whence they had originated. No doubt it was via the thick woolly fleece of the hill sheep in which they had been unwittingly transported into the rickety old shelter in the first place.

With teeth chattering, and trembling from tip of nose to tip of tail, it took only a matter of a few seconds to wash away the dreadful fleas from their bodies and, not a second longer than was necessary did they leap from the ice cold *shower* for fear of perishing beneath the flow as they *took off* at full speed up the moorland path to dry out their soaking skins in the early morning sunshine.

A little over two miles to the north of their present position lay the nearest of the pine woods which surround the old town of Alnwick but, to a small animal such as a red squirrel, this represented a distance of about two hundred miles for their little legs to cover so there was still a very long way for the two Redcoat brothers to go before they were safe in the company of their own family and friends.

In one of these pine woods, Duke and Duchess Redcoat were extremely anxious about their two missing sons for nothing more had been heard about them since the last report from the two passing crows about the two red squirrels they had seen in the tree tops way over the moor to the south and, despite several visits to the woodside wildlife café, there were no other sightings reported.

Duchess feared the worst for her two sons but Duke would hear none of such negative talk and scolded her for her lack of confidence in Rusty and Len. Ever the eternal optimist, Duke strongly believed that all would be fine and he was terribly sad that he was unable to venture out into the wild moor himself to find the two youngsters because the terrible injuries he had suffered at the talons of Buzz Buzzard had left him extremely weak and in no fit condition to undertake such a hazardous journey. Even so, in his heart he knew that both his sons would return safely but 'when' was the question he could not answer.

Dukes' instructions had gone out to each and every travelling creature to keep a sharp lookout for any sign of the Redcoat brothers and all Duke, and Duchess, could do was to wait patiently for some positive feedback.

About two hundred *animal miles* away to the south, Rusty and Len had managed to thoroughly dry their saturated bodies following their *moorland shower* but they now faced the biggest problem of all since meeting up almost two whole days ago.

Their frightful experiences of the last twelve hours had drained every gram of energy from their bodies as the two weary, and terribly hungry, red squirrels squatted down below some overhanging heather to contemplate their next plan of action which was, 'where to find food in this desolate expanse of wild countryside'?

'An old rustic sheep pen similar to the one where Rusty and Len sought shelter from the rain'

Chapter Eight

IS THIS THE LAST LAP ?

Hunger pangs drove the two Redcoat brothers further up the hillside in search of food. This wild, barren, landscape was definitely not red squirrel country so Rusty and Len Redcoat had to be content with any small scraps of food they could find and, so far, this only amounted to some meagre portions of lichen which they had to scrape from any boulders they came across on their journey.

As they paused to rest their tired legs, Len was forced to confess to his brother that he was hopelessly lost and way off course if they were to find their injured father Duke whom he still believed to be resting up in the rabbit warren recovering from his terrible injuries following his battle with Buzz Buzzard.

Rusty was not so sure their father would still be lying low in that rabbit hole because he knew this would expose him to extreme danger where, because of his wounds, he would not be able to defend himself, especially against any member of the sharp nosed Reynard Fox or Wally Weasel family who could smell an injured animal several miles away if the wind was blowing in the right direction.

It was now Rusty's firm belief that Duke Redcoat, their father, had at least made an attempt to return to the Redcoat family territory in the woods around Alnwick. Whether he had been successful in reaching home safely Rusty was not to know but he had the utmost confidence in his father's ability and the very thought of Duke perishing out on the wild moors did not enter Rusty's head.

Instead, Rusty insisted they press on upwards because he wanted to find the highest vantage point from which to survey their position. He also knew there was a good chance he would find a source of food which had to be their top priority and secondly, he would be able to plot a route which would take them downhill almost all the way home.

Within a few minutes Rusty spotted the skeleton frame of an old dead, solitary, Elm tree which had been a well known landmark on this part of the moor for a great many years. His eager call to Len spurred his brother on at greater speed and neither hesitated until they were both crouching low in the heather close to the gnarled old trunk of the dead Elm. This same old relic had also served countless generations of the different owl families as a night time perch from which to seek out their prey in the dark.

Rusty gave very firm instructions to his brother that he would play the roll of sentry to look out for any signs of danger while he would seek out the highest branch to conduct his survey without fear of being carried off by some marauding killers such as Gus Goshawk or Buzz Buzzard.

The sharp eyed Rusty, when given the all clear signal from his brother, sped to the very top branch where, within a matter of seconds, his telescopic eyes had recorded a clear picture of the whole panoramic view which he could see from his lofted position which was soon transferred to his memory bank !

Being sure he had not missed a single important detail, Rusty took a final look all around then scampered down to ground level at amazing speed.

As they sat under cover, Rusty gabbled excitedly to Len, telling him of all he had seen, even to the sighting of The Croft, far off to the south which he instantly recognised by the distinct shape of the roof tops and the blue smoke from a log fire curling up from the chimney pot.

Further to the east he had also spotted a human figure accompanied by a dog which Rusty believed to be Kevan, father of Sonny, who had saved his life and looked after him so lovingly for several months, but he could not be absolutely sure because they were so very, very far away.

As on other occasions, the long dry stone wall featured prominently along the foot of the hillside and Rusty knew he would have no trouble at all in reaching it but, it was still a long way off.

One other special feature intrigued Rusty in particular and this was a large stone building, more westwards from their present position, where several well worn tracks snaked from all parts of the moor right up to the front of the building.

This was actually the ruins of an old cottage, once occupied by generations of hill shepherds of many years ago, but was clearly in a very neglected condition, yet the roof was still intact. It was not so much the old building which interested Rusty but the small trees and bushes in the garden area at the front of the old hillside cottage. The red squirrel's extra sense which tells them that food is close by was *ringing tiny* bells in Rusty's brain and he knew this mysterious signal must be followed up, first and foremost.

Off they scampered, heading for cover of the light brown bracken further up the hillside to give them camouflage as they travelled. Low cloud also helped

'The old derelict cottage on Alnwick Moor'

to disguise their presence because it is the bright sunlight which transforms the animal's normal, dull rusty, colour into the bright, flame like, red from whence all red squirrels get their name. There is a remarkable transformation when the sun seems to act as a *spotlight* to show off the creature's brilliant coat but not always to those who appreciate the brilliance for, there are those who keep a sharp lookout for this wonderful red coat when searching for a meal !

Together they moved swiftly across the moor with Rusty in the lead. The torrential rain of the night before served to remove any red squirrel scent on the well worn sheep path but what both Rusty and his brother did not realise was that two distinct sets of footprints were being laid down in the wet mud which would so easily be recognised by some prowling predator and, guess what ? Yes, spot on ! Vicky Vixen Redcoat had returned to the *ramshackled* sheep shelter to sleep off her exertions of the long wet night and did not miss the tell-tale signs of eight tiny footprints in the mud !

Caution was the name of the game as the two Redcoat brothers made their way in the general direction of the old shepherd's cottage, not wanting to be caught out in open countryside.

As they journeyed on they were constantly noting all possible hiding places and escape routes as a matter of natural instinct. Without this extra-special in built safety attitude, the life of any red squirrel would not see them reach their first, half yearly, birthday.

Rusty was quick to observe strange hoof prints in the still damp mud as they travelled along which put his alarm system on high alert as did his brother who, as if by telepathy, recognised the tension in Rusty's movements as they proceeded with extreme caution.

Their careful approach was not careful enough as they spooked a Curlew feeding nearby. The two travelling redcoat brothers instantly took cover as the big startled bird took flight, uttering it's weird, warbling, call as it glided down the hillside to find another peaceful place to feed.

Moving on, the sight of the old chimney stack on the roof of the derelict cottage became visible against the sky and Rusty guided Len into the thick bracken where they separated to look for any sign of danger as each went their separate way, following the line of the dilapidated garden wall. After a couple of minutes they met up at a point where the original garden gate used to be where, only with tail movements did they signal to each other the fact that they had recognised the presence of strange animals inside the old garden.

Cautious as ever, the pair moved stealthily over towards a gap in the wall where, to their utter amazement, there were four of the strangest animals they had ever seen in their lives before, stretched out in the grass and all chewing some *invisible food* just as the hill sheep do and seemingly, without a care in the whole world.

Rusty was instantly aware that the strange hoof prints in the mud were made by these equally strange animals.

"Whatever can they be?" Len questioned his brother with just a quizzical look in his eyes ? "I think they're called *Boats*" answered Rusty but Len was quick to reply by telling his brother that *Boats* are things that humans play with on the water and qualified his statement by saying, " Because I saw them once when I followed the river in search of food and human children were playing games with *Boats* on the water, so those shaggy creatures can't be *Boats*".

"They're *Coats*" challenged Len but Rusty would have none of it because he was very familiar with coats because he'd even travelled on a long journey with Sonny in a coat pocket and, what's more, he had chewed holes in coat pockets to see just where he was going. Suddenly the name came to mind as he leaned over to whisper in his brother's ear, "They are called Goats" not wanting the fierce leader with the long hairy beard to overhear him talking !

"I remember seeing them briefly on the *mystery box* in Sonny's bedroom" but suddenly lost interest in the strange creatures as his eyes had now focussed on a rare crop of ripe black berries, known otherwise as brambles, growing way up over the top of the old garden wall and, before Len realised what was happening, Rusty had made a headlong dash into the undergrowth, drooling at the mouth at the very thought of a delicious, juicy, breakfast.

In about *five seconds flat* the two starving, and much bedraggled, Redcoat brothers were in amongst the over ripe fruit, cramming the delicious berries into their mouths as quick as they could gather them from the thorny stems. In about another sixty seconds their facial features had suddenly been transformed by the dark red, to almost blue as the juice of the ripe brambles which had stained their mouths, noses, yes, and even whiskers as they gorged themselves, quite unconcerned about anything else going on around them.

Front paws likewise changed colour and snow white breast and belly also became stained as they travelled from branch to branch seeking out the ripest fruit, oblivious of the sharp thorns which penetrated the soles of their feet as well as knees, elbows and even backsides, for which they would soon be very sorry.

Mixed in with the brambles were the rosiest fruits of all. These are the fruit of the rose bush called *rose hips* and Len was quick to advise his brother not to attempt to eat the seeds with horrible *whiskers* from inside the rose hips, having been well advised earlier by his wise father Duke when out on a recent feeding trip.

"Those terrible seeds can stick in your throat" he called to his brother "and no way can they be removed, NO WAY, so be very careful or else you will choke to death" at which Rusty promptly dropped his prize possession, not wanting to suffer a horrible death. Len however, was skilfully peeling off the sweet tasting skin from his fourth rose hip and soon the unwanted clumps of *hairy* seeds were dropping to the ground which did not go unnoticed by the ever hungry Goat family below.

Rusty had never before tasted anything so sweet as these rose hips and soon developed the knack of peeling off the delectable, fleshy skin with ease but the thorns of the ancient rose bush were even more painful than those of the brambles and now that their hunger pangs had been taken care of, each brother had to carefully pluck out the many thorns from the hide of each other which caused them to wince and giggle at the same time as they extracted each *tiny dagger* expertly with their front teeth.

Ever watchful for any sign of danger, Rusty had seen the antics of the Goats below when Len was busy removing the tiny barbs from his skin. The Goats wasted no time at all gobbling up any of the ripe fruit which fell to ground and they seemed to swallow whole the dreadful rose hip seed pods without any trouble at all in fact, they simply devoured the thorn laden twigs and leaves as well as if their tongues, and throats, were made of leather !

What Rusty spotted next almost caused him to lose his balance, such was the total delight at the sight of the large, fruit laden, bush which he spotted over in the opposite corner of the derelict garden, for they were none other than the most favourite, delicious, scrumptious, mouth watering and tastiest of all the wild red squirrel's food, that being the HAZEL NUT.

There is nothing quite like a hazel nut to send a red squirrel into raptures of delight than to crack open the hard, brittle shell, which they perform with great skill, to savour the tastiest morsel of all, that being the kernel which is contained within, for there is more nutrition in a single hazel nut than the seeds of a dozen large pine cones.

With a hop, skip and half a dozen jumps, Len showed his brother a clean pair of heels as he sped off in the direction of the hazel bush which was absolutely laden with ripe nuts. Len's first action was to select the ripest nuts of all, easily detected because of their rich brown colour, where he cleverly stuffed one into each pouch inside his cheeks and a third clenched firmly in his teeth then made his way down to the ground to seek out a convenient place to bury his *new found treasure* in the thick tufts of grass close to the old garden wall.

Rusty was curious as to what his brother was up to. The only time he had savoured these delicious nuts was when Sonny had brought them to his cage when in captivity at the Croft, never dreaming that they actually grew on bushes.

In a flash, Len had returned to explain to his bewildered brother just why it was necessary to bury some of the nuts. "This is to store them safely as an emergency food supply" Len told his brother. "Besides, there are far too many here for us to eat so we must save some for winter time".

"I know that Len but we may never, ever return to this place again and certainly not in winter" was Rusty's smart reply to which Len retorted, "No matter, these buried nuts may save the life of some wandering red squirrel in the future..

"What on earth are you doing now?" Rusty asked as he watched Len twirling a ripe nut in his front paws.

"This is a test to see if there is a nut inside the shell" Len told him. "You don't want to waste time and energy cracking open or burying a nut if there in nothing inside, do you" was Len's answer. "You have missed out on so much since you disappeared from our woodland home" Len told his brother who, despite all his doubts, was now on his way to ground with a mouthful of nuts, just to show Len that he was an understanding brother !

Neither Rusty nor Len fully realised the other importance of burying hazel nuts still inside the shell. Those nuts which are forgotten about will eventually seed and grow into young hazel saplings come springtime, if they are lucky enough to escape the ever hungry mouths of the hill sheep and wild goats, then they would finally produce the hazel bushes of the future, just as mother nature intended.

Soon the two intrepid brothers were taking their fill of nuts as they scampered through the branches to find the biggest and ripest nuts on display but their antics caused many of the ripe nuts to fall to the ground below which, also, did not go unnoticed by Herdi and Gerdi Goat who very soon led their two young offspring, *kids* to be precise, to an unexpected feast in the grass beneath the hazel bushes.

Herdi was the Chief of the herd of wild moorland goats, as his very name implies, and right now he was taking care of his partner Gerdi and her two *kids* now foraging in the tufted grass below. The crunching sound of the goats chewing the nuts caused both Rusty and Len some concern as they perched well above these strange creatures for they were not to know that goats have stomachs like *food mixers* and can digest *almost anything* !

Herdi especially, was a massive brute, well over a metre and a half tall and sporting a pair of evil looking horns which protruded from the top of his broad forehead and sloped backwards over his powerful shoulders, lethal weapons indeed. He also sported a long straggly beard almost the same colour as that of the red coated squirrel.

Although the sight of the goats caused the two hungry red squirrels some curiosity, neither Rusty nor Len felt in any danger as they were well above ground, *or so they thought*, as they continued to munch on their hazel nut lunch.

Herdi, in particular, was none too happy when the tasty nuts stopped falling to ground and, not wanting to be deprived of such a delicious meal, soon *eyed up* a way to reach the nuts on the higher branches. He simply rose up on his hind legs, as if winched from above by *some invisible rope*, and hooked his front paws over one of the lower branches where his sheer weight brought the branch down to a manageable level for Gerdi and her two *kids* to strip off any remaining nuts, and leaves.

Once the branch had been stripped clean, Herdi let go and the pliable branch whipped back violently, almost knocking the two red squirrels from their perch above. Both Rusty and Len ignored this action as they were too intent on filling their bellies when Herdi grabbed yet another fruit laden branch which just happened to be the same branch upon which Rusty was sitting, eating another hazel nut which he held in his front paws.

As Herdi pulled down on the heavy bough he soon realised that, as strong as he was, the branch was too 'slippy' to hold firm and was forced to let go. With a sudden 'WHOOSH' the branch sprang upwards in a flash and the *whiplash* catapulted Rusty ever on upwards. Len heard the 'WEEEEEEAHAHAH' as his brother sailed through the air, over his head, and cleared the old garden wall by six feet or more to land out of sight in the heather outside the old garden.

As a natural reaction, Rusty had spread his arms and legs in mid air, just like a *freefall sky diver*, still holding on to the hazel nut with his teeth, to land belly down on the thick carpet of heather. The abrupt landing knocked the wind out of him but no more than that as he gasped to recover his breath and, at the same time, looked around to find his nearest means of escape which just happened to be the old dilapidated garden wall.

Just as quickly as he scaled the wall, Len had done likewise from the other side where they met together below an overhanging hazel branch from which they nimbly climbed to the very top twigs, both very excited and mightily relieved that no serious injuries had occurred.

They chased and hugged among the topmost branches with true red squirrel *brotherly love* as Herdi, Gerdi and their *two* kids continued their hazel nut *picnic* below as if nothing at all had happened.

The whole episode, however, had not gone un-noticed. Sitting atop the old chimney stack, the two brothers of the Jackdaw family, namely Jack and Matt, had silently observed the scene below with typical Jackdaw curiosity and were not going to waste even one second as they *took flight* and headed north towards Alnwick and the woodland *wildlife café* where they knew the tale they had to tell would make them heroes in and around the territory of the Redcoat squirrel family home.

Finally, unable to eat even half a nut more, Rusty led his brother up to the very top of a dangerous chimney stack so they could plot the last lap of their journey together. Len soon recognised the area where he had left his father Duke injured inside the abandoned rabbit hole and also pointed out to Rusty certain familiar landmarks which, they both agreed, would lead them back to Redcoat territory, hopefully in the company of their injured father.

The sun peeped out from a hole in the clouds high above to signal mid-day and Rusty suggested they both take a nap before setting off on their homeward journey. *Forty winks* around mid-day is a regular habit with most red squirrels, especially red squirrels with a *bellyfull* of blackberries and hazel nuts !

Soon they were exploring the roof space inside the derelict cottage where they discovered some old nest material tucked away in the top of the wall, tight beneath the slates above. Satisfied that this was as safe a place as could be found, the two exhausted brothers were bedded down out of sight and, with their *emergency alarm systems* switched on, both fell into a deep sleep.

Way back down the hillside, in the *ramshackled* sheep shelter, another creature was taking her regular daily nap and she too had her own alert system switched on, for, even in her sleep, Vicky Vixen Reynard had only one subject on her mind and that was the possibility of having a couple of tasty red squirrels for supper !

'Rear of the old derelict house where wild goats, foxes, starlings and owls frequented'

Chapter Nine

WHATEVER NEXT ?

Rusty and his brother Len were utterly exhausted due to loss of sleep during the previous two nights as they lay *out for the count* below the slates in the eaves of the derelict shepherd's cottage way up on the side of Alnwick Moor.

The sun had now dropped far down in the west leaving only a couple of hours before dusk, not enough daylight to continue on their journey back to Redcoat territory as there was no guarantee of another safe resting place for the night ahead.

Almost in a trance, the two sleepy brothers were totally oblivious to anything going on around them for which they would have received a severe rollicking from their father Duke had he been there to witness the total disregard for their own safety. The old derelict cottage was a well used abode for almost every predator around, day and night, so much so that it would not take long for their presence to be detected, putting their lives at risk once again.

Meanwhile, Jack and Matt Jackdaw had lost no time returning to the forest to break the news to all who gathered beside the woodland wildlife café at Oliver and Isobel's place and soon the whole neighbourhood was buzzing with incessant chatter about the definite sighting of the two Redcoat brothers up at the old ruined cottage on the hillside, far away up on the moor.

In less than fifteen minutes, the tremendous news had spread deep inside the woodland where the whole family, and relatives, of Redcoats were busy feasting in a giant oak tree which was laden with ripe acorns. It was none other than Nutty Nuthatch who, having heard Jack and Matt Jackdaw's report, had streaked through the trees to break the news to Milly and Yum who in turn performed the most fantastic, death defying circus act up in the highest branches, soon to be joined by every red squirrel present in what can only be described as a wild frenzy of emotion when the entire old oak tree came alive with the mad, hair raising antics of more than a dozen 'trapeze artistes' in concert, celebrating the marvellous news as only red squirrels know how.

The speed at which they performed their celebratory chase was as if they were each charged with electricity as they twisted, leaped and almost flew at times, all at such an alarming, breakneck speed, it was a miracle indeed that not one ended up injured, or worse, on the ground.

Only one solitary figure remained motionless as he watched the frantic celebrations with more pride than ever in his long, illustrious, life before. This of course was none other than Duke Redcoat, father of the two intrepid brothers Rusty and Len and leader of the whole red squirrel community in the woodlands around Alnwick.

The injuries he had sustained at the claws and horrible beak of Buzz Buzzard during his quest to rescue his long lost son Rusty, and which he had no other option but to pass the responsibility on to his other son Len, were still not sufficiently healed to allow him to move freely and besides, he was far too old to be *gallivanting* around in the tree tops like some mad young thing.

The news was just what Duke Redcoat had expected because he had complete faith in his two sons and always believed they would come to no harm but, just a tiny little niggle at the back of Duke's mind told him not to celebrate too early because, and after all, they were not safely home yet !

Meanwhile, back at the old derelict cottage, two little rusty red coated creatures began to stir following their marathon sleepover, terribly thirsty and somewhat a *wee bit peckish !!*

At first, Rusty had to shake his head in order to remember what had happened before he had fallen into a deep sleep but it was not until he banged his head on the slates above did he become wide awake. Len, in the meantime, shuffled sluggishly as if in a daze but soon gathered his wits about him when Rusty scolded him for being so lazy.

"You can talk" scoffed Len, "you've just woken up yourself so stop bullying me"

"I'm not bullying you" answered Rusty, "but I think we've slept far too long and left it too late to travel any further today so we must take stock of our present position and make a plan for tomorrow." With that said, Rusty looked around to find an easy route up onto the roof above but, ever cautious in case of any hidden danger.

They soon made their way through the window opening and scaled over the spout onto the capping stones on the gable end and finally ended up on top of the chimney stack all in about twenty seconds.

Len was first to recognise their exact position for he promptly identified the spot where his father Duke had engaged Buzz Buzzard in battle when

62

on their way to rescue Rusty. Len even pointed out to his brother the very location where he still believed his father to be laying up, recovering from his wounds.

Rusty was quick to tell Len that he did not believe their father would still be down inside that rabbit hole for the simple reason it would prove to be too dangerous and Len had to agree.

'The wild goat family' (by kind permission of Matt O'Brien)

From their vantage on top of the chimney stack, it was soon evident that Herdi and Gerdi Goat and their two kids had settled down beneath the bushes in the back garden as all four animals were lying down comfortably, almost out of sight, and Rusty believed they were resting after their feast of hazel nuts. " Fancy eating hazel nuts whole" Rusty quietly mentioned to Len who responded with a "YUK, however do they do it" ?

Of course neither realised, or even knew, that the stomach of a goat is capable of digesting almost anything ! All four goats seemed so content as they continually chewed away at nothing in particular, as is the way of all goats.

Len, having spent more time than his brother in the woodlands around Alnwick, was quick to identify certain landmarks which he pointed out to Rusty and, of the two brothers, Rusty was first to formulate a plan in his mind and knew, almost instantly, the route they would have to take but, they would not be leaving the deserted old cottage until very early next morning. Hopefully !

Ever mindful of their need to drink, Rusty led the way down to ground and soon found a small pool, more like the tiny pond, in the corner of the overgrown garden where they both took their fill before returning to the lofty perch to carefully scan the countryside around.

The barren hillside was laced with many well worn sheep, and goat, tracks coming and going in all directions. "We must study and memorise these paths carefully" Rusty told Len "in case we become separated on the last lap of our journey" and Len simply squeaked a nonchalant answer of agreement knowing just how easy it was to get lost on this desolate moor.

Way down the hillside, the raucous noise of a startled Cock Pheasant in flight caused the two inquisitive red squirrel brothers to sit up and take notice. Not only did the pheasant take wing but several Red Grouse also flew away in haste as two human figures suddenly came into sight way down below but there was no doubt at all in Rusty's mind that these two young humans were on their way to explore the deserted cottage, of that he was very sure. Having had far more experience of human behaviour than Len, Rusty's whiskers began to twitch !

Len instantly recognised the twitching whisker signal as that of imminent danger but their curiosity kept them transfixed to the old chimney stack. Every now and then one of the young men seemed to fire some missile or other into the bracken, or heather, from a peculiar weapon and it was this action which caused the wild moorland birds to take flight.

Suddenly, Len recalled a tale his Scottish uncle, Big Bob Blacktail, had told him about this strange and dangerous weapon when he himself had once been the target of some marauding humans and was lucky to have escaped with his life.

Suddenly, a missile flew close to his head with a 'Whoosh'. Len told Rusty they must take cover immediately as their lives would definitely be in danger if these youths spotted them.

Len racked his brain to remember the name of the weapon which Uncle Big Bob Blacktail had described but, he was too busy to recall as he chased after his brother who was already on his way to take cover inside the old deserted cottage.

'Cat or Catty' something or other flashed through Len's mind for he dearly wanted to let his brother know how knowledgeable he was about such things. "It's a Catapult" Len told Rusty as the proper name suddenly came to mind. "What is" ? asked Rusty, his mind more intent on securing a safe hiding place, "Well, that thing you know. The thing those young humans are using as a weapon. It's called a Catapult because Uncle Big Bob Blacktail told me, so it must be true" Len retorted as he perched alongside his brother up in the corner of the eaves beneath the roof slates.

Their entry inside the old derelict cottage had caused a big flock of roosting Starlings to flutter and twitch excitedly in alarm but they soon settled down on the timber spars where they chirped and twittered none stop, each bird was determined to have his, or her, voice heard. One by one they appeared to cease their incessant blether and began to preen their feathers in a most particular fashion, making sure that each and every feather received the required amount of grooming.

The two curious red squirrels could not help but notice just how beautiful was the plumage of these widely travelled birds and, of course, it was vitally necessary for them to keep their feathers in perfect order to enable them to perform the magic flight patterns for which Starlings are famous all over the world.

In the still of the late afternoon the silence was suddenly broken once again by the sound of human voices close to the old cottage and the distinct thud of a propelled missile striking the outer wall which caused each and every Starling to strike up a most nervous chorus of *shrieks* and high pitched whistles.

The noise was amplified ten times up in the roof space where, as another missile struck the slates above, pandemonium broke out among the flock of Starlings as they sought a means of escape.

The whirring of about two hundred pairs of wings was like a wild gale in winter as each bird fought it's own way to freedom when they streamed out of the old building by way of the window opening just below the roof spars.

Silence suddenly descended on the old cottage for a brief moment while four tufted ears were straining to detect the slightest sound which would warn them of possible danger. Twitching whiskers told the two alert red squirrels that all was not well as they both detected the approaching footsteps of the young humans, even in the grass below. Rusty suddenly found himself thinking about his dear friend Sonny who had rescued him from the wrecked drey and mentioned to himself that "Sonny would not be as clumsy as these two interlopers" which were his thoughts as the two boys outside communicated in whispers.

They may as well have shouted from the tops of their voices as far as Rusty and Len were concerned because they could hear every word very clearly. "You go 'round the other side and I'll take the doorway" one of the boys uttered as the late afternoon sun cast a moving shadow across the door opening. Len nudged his brother gently to point out the movement of the shadow below when, from the window opening opposite, the head and shoulders of the second youth appeared, catapult at the ready !!

Both Rusty and Len now had a clear sight of the armed youth who suddenly drew back his left arm and, with his right arm fully extended forward, released a lethal missile up into the roof space above the ceiling rafters with an almighty TWANG.

The power of the projectile caused it to ricochet, firstly off one spar then another as it struck the underside of the slates and fell harmlessly to the floor below.

Immediately, the young human with the catapult vaulted through the window opening, retrieved the missile from the floor and promptly re-armed his weapon. From the opposite side, the second youth appeared through the open doorway armed with an assortment of sticks which he deftly flung upwards, one at a time, between the ceiling joists, aimed at nothing in particular as, once again, another missile was launched from the catapult with another violent TWANG.

The velocity of this rounded stone caused it to hit the angle of the main timber support and fly like a bullet from a gun clean across the space in the roof where it struck the slates only ten inches or so above the heads of the pair of terrified squirrels. It passed straight through the slate roof allowing the bright evening sun to blaze through, like the beam from a powerful torch, directly onto the two frightened creatures.

Red squirrels wag their tails for a variety of reasons and in this case it was Len who gave their position away by wagging his tail in fear. From the top of the stone wall the movement of Len's tail was like a waving flag in the bright beam of sunlight which now shone through the hole in the slate roof above. This was instantly spotted by the sharp eyed youth with the catapult who wasted no time at all in launching another missile from his primitive, but lethal weapon.

This time the stone flew directly upwards to crash, yet again, through the slates close by, too close for comfort, as Rusty pulled his brother closer in to the angle of the old roof so as to remain out of sight but now both youths were terribly excited at the sight of live animals up in the roof space as yet another missile whistled its way in the direction of the two red squirrels who were now in mortal danger.

More sticks were flung up in their direction as the second raider attempted to scale the wall to reach a higher vantage point from which to fire his catapult with more desired effect. A quick glance over the edge told Rusty that they were now likely to lose their lives if they remained where they were when an almighty scream echoed through the empty building.

A huge shadowy figure now filled the door opening from where the early evening sun resembled the flames of an enormous fire and the silhouette of the massive and powerful Herdi Goat suddenly appeared. He was not too happy at having his early evening nap disturbed but, moreover, he wanted to make sure that none of his family was in any danger. His very presence was enough to frighten a grown man, or several grown men come to that, as Herdi pawed the floor in front of him and snorted a clear warning to the occupants in the room that he was not going to tolerate any more of this bedlam being created by the two excited youths.

The young human on the ground, the one armed with sticks and dressed in baggy trousers, froze instantly with fear, as if temporarily paralysed, at the sight of the monster in the doorway before he dropped his weapons and took a flying leap through the window opening. A protruding rusty nail, sticking up from the old window sill, was to prove the undoing of his attempt to escape as it ripped one of his trouser legs, almost the full length, before he fell headlong onto the grass below and straight into the very powerful hands of Kevan the Gamekeeper who just happened to be on his rounds.

'The rusty nail in the old window frame which caused problems for one of the hooligans'

Now up in the rafters, the second young trouble maker with ill intent was distracted by the scream of his friend and the strange snorting sounds below, nearly fell through the ceiling joists with fright and realised he was well and truly trapped.

All previous display of bravado suddenly abandoned the youth as he trembled with fear at the terrifying sight of Herdi Goat still standing guard in the doorway and, what's more, there was no sign of his human companion. The youth up in the rafters had not escaped the notice of the observant Herdi as he continued to paw and snort to make his powerful presence known.

Way up in the opposite corner cowered the two Redcoat brothers, totally speechless at what they were witnessing before their very eyes but content now to stay put. The timely arrival of Herdi Goat had definitely saved their skins but they were now eager to see what was going to happen to the young human with the catapult, sitting astride a large beam only a matter of four to five yards away.

No longer was the youth in the roof space interested in maiming the poor defenceless creatures opposite with his lethal weapon. His cowardly reaction was to shed tears of fear for he fully realised that his position was positively hopeless as there appeared to be no means of escape from the dreaded Herdi Goat.

Now that all the boldness had deserted him, the trembling youth was about to pass out with fear when Herdi suddenly decided that his presences was no longer required and promptly did an about turn and moved off to rejoin Gerdi and the Kids.

Hardly able to believe his good fortune, the still trembling young human stuffed the catapult into his trouser pocket and, in one agile movement, swung down to ground from the rafters. Not wanting to risk bumping into Herdi Goat the youngster chose the self same route of escape as his companion, that being through the window opening which he deftly manoeuvred and, just like his companion, ended up being held by the scruff of the neck by the strong arm of Kevan the Gamekeeper.

At the sound of Kevan's voice "Now what have we here?" Rusty's heart skipped a beat with surprise and sheer joy.

As he hugged his brother in a gesture of relief he also warned Len not to utter as much as a squeak until he gave him the all clear.

The all familiar voice of Kevan was almost too much for Rusty who desperately wanted to let Sonny's father know he was present inside the old derelict house but allowed his head to overrule his heart as he sat close to his brother while they listened to the stern voice of Kevan the Gamekeeper down below.

What Rusty did not realise was that Kevan had already spotted the neatly split fresh hazel nut shells in the corner of the derelict garden which told the wise and experienced gamekeeper that at least one red squirrel was hiding in the deserted cottage and that he was certain that Rusty Redcoat was not too far away !

"And just what do you think you two young hoodlums are up to causing all this commotion and damage" ? he questioned the boys. "Nothing mister" was the reply uttered timidly by one of them. "Nothing" exclaimed Kevan. "You call smashing the roof slates with a catapult nothing" Kevan asked of them but received no reply. "I'm going to release my hold on the two of you but one attempt to do a bunk and you'll find your ankles being nipped quite smartly by Terry here" as Kevan took out his notebook and pencil to record the names and addresses of the two young offenders for future reference.

Rusty was astonished to hear of Terry the Terrier's presence for he had no idea that the dog, who had sniffed him out after he had torn Sonny's bed to bits when he was in captivity over in The Croft, was so very close by.

"We mustn't give our presence away" Rusty whispered in his brother's ear. "I'll tell you why later on" as the voice of Kevan the Gamekeeper continued down below in a very stern manner.

Believing he was just as astute as his master Kevan, Terry the Terrier had sniffed the familiar scent of Rusty, and another red squirrel, as he poked his head through the door opening. His tail began to wag in excitement just as it had done a long time ago when he had detected the little red culprit who had caused all that terrible damage to Sonny's bed.

"I'm going to confiscate this catapult and hand it in at the Police Station to-gether with your names and addresses and, if I catch either of you trespassing up here again, you will have Terry here to contend with ! Now off you go the pair of you" uttered Kevan.

No sooner had the two miscreants moved off when Terry the Terrier began to stamp his authority with his familiar triumphant barking, familiar to Rusty that is, for the very smart little dog was not only telling the two young humans what would happen to them next time they met, he was also actually telling his master Kevan that he had detected the powerful scent of his old adversary, Rusty Redcoat, in and around the old derelict cottage !

Unable to curtail his urge to see Kevan and his faithful terrier dog once again, Rusty crept stealthily towards the hole in the slates, recently breached by a missile from that terrible catapult, and eased his head up slowly to peer over the edge of the roof. There he could clearly see Kevan striding downhill, his favourite walking stick in his hand and his faithful dog, Terry the Terrier, with his tail still wagging frantically, at his heel.

Rusty was full of emotion at the sight of Sonny's father and his dog but what happened next was quite unexpected. Kevan, ever so casually, glanced backwards over his shoulder, just in time to see the tiny little red head disappear below the slates

With another sly grin to himself, Kevan marched on, having been aware of Rusty Redcoat's presence at the old derelict cottage, before his encounter with the two wayward youths, for he could read the signs and antics of his four legged partner Terry as clear as words from a book. After all, you don't get to be Gamekeeper of the Year if you walk about the countryside with eyes and ears closed !!!

Terry the Terrier's antics had simply proved what Kevan had already deduced for the two sets of red squirrel's footprints in the mud on the moorland track had not gone unnoticed.

Rusty could no longer contain himself as he poured out even more stories of his days in captivity to Len who listened intently to more *hair raising* tales. Rusty had, of course, told Len previously about some of his escapades when they were holed up in the dry stone wall on the first night of their reunion but the tale about the damaged bed and Terry the Terrier took Len's breath away.

"We have no other option but to stay here yet another night" Rusty mentioned to Len who detected a note of disappointment in his brother's voice. Len knew all too well just how much Rusty missed his family, in particular Milly and Yum, and also agreed that, for their own safety, another night's lodgings in this old deserted cottage was unavoidable as the first scout of the Starling flock flew back in to check the place over and send some sort of signal to the others that all was O.K.

As the Starlings returned in twos and threes to take up their own individual roosting place, Len followed Rusty down to quench their thirst at the pool in the corner of the garden. Len was quick to lead his brother to the hidden stash of hazel nuts he had buried previously to show Rusty just what a smart brother he was as they each stuffed several of the buried nuts into the pouches on either side of their mouth before scampering back to their safe refuge.

The sun finally dropped out of sight behind the hill to the west and darkness took over the barren moorland once again as Rusty and Len Redcoat settled down on the stone ledge to devour their hazel nut supper. The heat of the autumn sun had warmed up the stones immediately beneath the slate roof which was to be a blessing for the two tired red squirrel brothers as they snuggled in to each other on the warm stone ledge to sleep. Down below on the spars the flock of tired Starlings twittered and fidgeted until, at last, they too drifted off into *Starling* slumberland.

Way down the side of the moor, one creature was now fully awake and following her nose up the well worn sheep and goat track. Vicky Vixen Reynard was on her regular night time prowl and the scent she was following was that of Rusty and Len Redcoat.

Mistress Vicky Reynard literally drooled at the mouth at the very thought of a tasty evening meal of red squirrel at long last when, at some distance from the deserted cottage, her long bushy red tail, with the distinct white tip, drooped in disappointment when another, and stronger, scent crossed her path and stopped her dead in her tracks.

This was the unmistaken scent of Herdi Goat and his family which put the fear of dread into Vicky Vixen Reynard for Herdi was one mean creature who would not tolerate any member of the Reynard clan anywhere near his precious family and, before morning would break, the sleeping occupants of the old deserted cottage were about to have their sleep interrupted once again, in no uncertain terms.

'Up in the roof space of the derelict cottage where Rusty and Len took shelter'

Chapter Ten

'SAT NAV NOSE'!!

A bird's eye view is that seen from above which is exactly what Ornie the Tawny Owl could see, yes, even in the dark, as he glided silently over Alnwick moor that evening.

With his night scope vision, and knowledge of his domain, he at first focussed on the old deserted cottage which, to Ornie's eye, glowed in the darkness and told the hunting owl that food was a plenty inside that old building because his long experience had taught him the exact night time signs of a flock of roosting starlings.

Furthermore, Ornie could clearly identify Herdi Goat and his family as they slept out in the open in the corner of the overgrown garden but an extra tawny owl sense told Ornie that there was a couple of extra *bodies* down there which he could not properly identify and which he would have to investigate later on!

His next sighting told Ornie of the presence of Vicky Vixen Reynard as she slinked her way slowly up the side of the moor to the south. Vicky was all too easy to detect, especially in the dark, because of the glow from her two green eyes, like fluorescent lights, which bobbed up and down as she travelled cautiously towards the deserted cottage and, to the wise old owl, Vicky Vixen shone like a beacon in the night.

Way over to the north, Ornie was able to spot yet another pair of green fluorescent eyes and they too told the wise old owl that another of the Reynard family was heading up the opposite side of Alnwick moor and it was heading straight for the old deserted cottage.

"There's a lot of interest in that place to-night" thought Ornie as he circled in the night sky effortlessly, intently focussed on the gloomy scene below.

It took Ornie a minute or two before he could put a name to the owner of the second pair of green fluorescent eyes. It had been many months since Ornie had seen 'Sat Nav Nose' Reynard over on this part of the moor and he very soon knew the specific reason for Sat Nav's presence.

The extremely wise night bird had calculated by the very fast pace at which Sat Nav Nose was travelling that it was not only food which was on the dog fox's mind at all and Ornie was quick to realise that Sat Nav Nose was coming courting because he had picked up the scent of Vicky Vixen Reynard, down wind of him, about two hours ago.

To pick up the scent of another fox is quite a natural thing for most foxes to do, but only if the wind is in the right direction or else there is a strong ground scent to follow however, Sat Nav Nose was well known for many miles around by the wildlife creatures for his extraordinary powers of detection.

It was for this very reason that he had been nicknamed Sat Nav Nose by none other than Kevan the Gamekeeper who had been after this crafty old predator fox for several years but it had always been the exceptional powers of detection by Sat Nav's extra sensitive nose which had helped him resist capture on many previous occasions.

To avoid any confusion, it has to be explained that the notorious Reynard fox family is a very large family indeed who, almost all, exist and operate on their own except for the mother fox when she has cubs to raise. Sat Nav Nose is the son of the elderly Ray Reynard and brother of Roxy Fox, both are far distant relatives of Vicky Vixen so now you know the Reynard family set up who inhabit the lands around Alnwick

Late into the night the two red squirrels were comfortably tucked in underneath the roof slates and sleeping soundly. Two sets of twitching whiskers were receiving invisible signals which, to the two young brothers, were not sufficiently strong to register in their sleepy heads as any sign of alarm.

Because of the imminent danger at ground level, as well as in the air, any adult red squirrel would have been wide awake by now but, for the two young Redcoat brothers, the pleasures of dreamland were not to be interrupted, especially when the whole of the Redcoat family were enjoying a fantastic picnic in the woods in the dreamy minds of Rusty and his brother Len !

Ornie the Tawny Owl had decided that a couple of tasty fat starlings would do nicely for his late evening meal and Vicky Vixen was positively drooling at the thought of a double helping of red squirrel which would be just perfect to take back to her two hungry cubs as she steadily plodded her way up the path on the south side of the moor.

The now faint scent from the pathway of the two Redcoat brothers was still strong enough to drive her forward with a purpose for she knew how

'Ornie the Tawny Owl. The wise old friend of Duke Redcoat'

easy it would be to grab the two red coated squirrels in the dark. They would be fast asleep she thought and of course, Vicky Vixen held the advantage because she too has night time vision just as well as Ornie the Tawny Owl. Meanwhile, about half a kilometre to the north, Sat Nav Nose too proceeded with a purpose as he trotted along with his nose in the air, also with the derelict cottage in mind, for it was in the light south westerly breeze that the strong scent of Vicky Vixen was borne across the bracken, right on to the end of Sat Nav's nose.

The derelict moorland cottage was now virtually under siege, from three different angles, by three different invaders, one each from the north and south, the other from above as Ornie swooped down from a great height with ghostly silence to alight upon the protruding chimney pot. Ornie had used this same manoeuvre many times before over the years and had very seldom failed in his quest for an evening meal.

'Unless I'm very much mistaken' thought Ornie 'my guess is that there are two red squirrels somewhere under this roof but, 'this is not the normal habitat for any of Duke Redcoat's relatives' he mused. Then he recalled all the gossip in and around Alnwick woodlands a few days ago about two missing red squirrels. 'My sensors tell me there are two sleeping *redcoats* close by but, exactly where, I am not quite sure'.

Starlings are not like red squirrels for they do not have sensitive whiskers with which to detect danger signs. Whatever it is they do possess by way of an early warning device was certainly switched on as one or two began to shuffle on the ceiling joists and the alarm signal was quickly passed to all the birds in the flock Their immediate unease became apparent as the shuffling increased and faint twitterings, no doubt in starling language, were now distinctly audible inside the old derelict cottage.

Two sets of whiskers began twitching like crazy as Rusty and Len lay fast asleep up on the stone ledge beneath the roof slates. The twitterings from the entire flock of starlings was becoming louder, with an agitated tone, in the black darkness of the roof space and it was, for sure, that the presence of Ornie the Tawny Owl outside on the chimney pot had been detected.

Rusty awoke with a start and, for several seconds, was unable to gather his wits about him having been in such a sound sleep. An instant feeling of unease caused him to give Len a nudge and he too was awakened from his deep slumber and almost fell from the narrow stone shelf as he began to stretch his cramped limbs. Rusty was quick to grab hold of his brother's fore paws in the gloom which caused Len to utter a startled squeak as he too was not yet fully awake.

The sudden movement by the two red squirrel brothers, and in particular Len's squeaky cry, was all it took to cause a wave of pandemonium to break out amongst the already startled flock of starlings. Believing that Ornie the Tawny Owl had entered the building they began to flutter about in the darkness and the previous quiet twittering was now a frantic screeching noise as they all sought to find some form of shelter from the invisible Ornie but unable to see anything at all in the blackness of the night.

The frightful noise of perhaps a hundred fluttering starlings was enough to unsettle Rusty and his brother. Rusty knew full well they were not the only cause of the panic among the flock of starlings but the noise they were creating prevented either Rusty, or Len, from detecting the presence, or movement, of any silent and menacing predator as they squeezed further down below the roof slates as far as they possibly could.

Rusty recalled his recent experience in the old barn back at The Croft when he created a dust storm with his wild and frantic antics on that particular afternoon and now he was on the receiving end of a similar happening, only this was ten times worse as the dust settled all over their bodies causing them to sneeze fitfully.

Both he and Len nipped their noses with fore paws to help prevent them from sneezing, which would surely give their position away, when the volume of the starling voices suddenly rose to a deafening crescendo as the fearful Ornie swept silently inside through the window opening below. Rusty distinctly heard two terrifying screams above all the others which told him, first of all, that two of the starlings had met their doom and secondly, that the night time invader was none other than Ornie the wise old Tawny Owl.

As if by some mysterious command, the flock of starlings suddenly ceased their cries of fear and began to find their own particular perch in the darkness and, once again settle down to get what sleep they could before taking off on their travels come the first light of dawn.

" Did you recognise that silent killer"? Rusty asked his brother. "No doubt at all who that was" replied Len.

"Thank goodness this flock of starlings is roosting in here or else it could so easily have been you or me, or maybe both of us, being carried off by that silent killer" whispered Rusty. Because they had been in such a sound sleep they really believed Ornie's huge talons would have grabbed them in the darkness as they slept and that would have been the end of the story but, they were not to know that red squirrels are not considered part of a Tawny Owl's menu !

" You know Len, we have both been incredibly stupid. We must learn to switch on our red squirrel alarm systems before going off to sleep." "I agree" said Len "but I was just too tired and did not think wisely".

"Me too" replied Rusty "but it could so easily have been us being devoured by Ornie the Tawny Owl and we must never, ever, make the same stupid mistake again". "I promise" said Len. "So do I" replied his brother. Promises, promises !!!

Little did they know that Ornie the Tawny Owl had no intention of killing the two red squirrel brothers. First of all, a red squirrel is far too big and ferocious for a Tawny Owl to tackle which is perhaps why red squirrel is not listed on Ornie Owl's diet sheet, or for any other owl come to that but, Rusty and Len were too young and inexperienced to have known that.

A faint glow appeared on the horizon to the east as the morning sun began to show its' presence once again. This faint glow was the signal to all the surviving starlings to take wing and fly off, to wherever, to seek their breakfast in the early morning light. With just a few chirps here and there, it was as if someone had given a silent signal to start a race, the whole flock took off together, minus two of their family of course, and within twenty seconds Rusty and Len found themselves quite alone. At least for the time being!

Sat Nav Nose was as happy as a *sand piper* as he loped his way towards the derelict cottage and the scent of Vicky Vixen was ever so much stronger in that *sat nav* nose of his. Vicky Vixen, on the other hand, was nearing the deserted cottage with only one thought on her mind, and that was NOT Sat Nav Nose Reynard, for she was *positively positive* that a red squirrel breakfast for herself and her two hungry cubs was to be found inside that cottage and she would have to be at her most cunning best if she was to succeed as she too loped onwards towards the old cottage with her nose close to the ground, completely unaware of the approaching dog fox nearby.

This time, and in total unison, the two Redcoat brothers sat *bolt* upright as their alarm systems sent out an instant danger signal. Rusty looked quizzically at his brother before venturing carefully out onto the eaves through the hole in the slates created yesterday by the youth with the catapult. The light was still rather gloomy as the sun had risen behind a bank of cloud on its journey upwards. Rusty made his way to a better vantage point, that being up on top of the chimney stack where, only a few moments earlier, had sat Ornie the Tawny Owl.

Len was soon crouching close by his brother. Two pairs of eyes are twice as good as one pair as they both scanned the misty countryside around them for the slightest sign of danger.

Hunger was a distraction for the two starving Redcoat brothers as each in turn spotted an approaching fox in the distance, one from the south side and another from the north. "This looks a bit *dodgy*" exclaimed Rusty "but we must try to take a drink and grab some of those hazels because we could well be trapped in here for a long time if those two killers manage to pick up our scent".

Len did not even think about a reply as he shot down to ground level in a flash leaving his brother a couple of seconds behind. They both, rather greedily, gulped down as much cool water from the spring in the old garden as they could hold then headed straight for the hazel bush to grab what nuts they could find.

They were just about to make their way back to the safety of the old deserted cottage roof when, around the corner, strolled Herdi Goat with his partner Gerdi, and their two kids, for they too needed to quench their thirst and, in so doing, blocked the way back to the cottage as they nonchalantly meandered along the pathway, taking up a position directly beneath the hazel bush.

Neither Rusty nor Len could utter a single word as their cheek pouches were stuffed with nuts but, glances and tail signals were sufficient to tell each other that the situation was very serious.

Rusty thought it would take forever for the four goats to quench their thirst at the tiny garden spring and was fearful that a sudden movement on their part would startle Herdi and his family and so the two redcoat brothers sat motionless as each goats drank their fill of moorland water.

All of a sudden, Herdi snorted an alarm call as he raised his mighty head and sniffed the air. Undoubtedly he had picked up the scent of one of the two foxes approaching as the direction of the wind had changed since the sun had made it's appearance. Herdi again snorted instructions to his family who nervously pushed their way below the hazel bush to seek protection in the angle of the old garden wall.

Herdi took up guard in front of his family with head bowed and snorting like a bull with eyes blazing as he pawed the ground in front of him in a defiant gesture.

Rusty removed the two hazel nuts from his mouth and whispered to Len that they would have to risk getting back inside the cottage. "If we stay out here there will be no escape at all, especially with two crafty foxes to deal with".

With cheeks bulging with nuts, Len nodded in agreement as, on Rusty's tail signal, they made their dash to safety while Herdi's mind was focussed on other matters and they were back inside the old cottage within five seconds. Stashing their hoard of hazel nuts safely on top of the stone ledge, Rusty led his brother, once again, up to the highest vantage point of the old chimney stack where they would at least be reasonably safe to observe the scene below. So intrigued were they at what they thought was about to happen, Rusty and Len did not realise they had instantly given away their presence as both Vicky Vixen and Sat Nav Nose immediately spotted their movements from two different positions.

Sat Nav Nose had already heard the threatening snorting of Herdi Goat and suddenly changed direction as he dashed across to intercept Vicky Vixen to warn her of Herdi's presence. With a quick rubbing of noses, Vicky at once recognised Sat Nav's high state of alert.

It was more than six hours since Sat Nav had eaten and, although he was solely intent on making a romantic acquaintance of Vicky Vixen in a more gentlemanly way, the hunger pangs now forced him to change his mind.

Now, it has to be understood that a single fox on a mission to find a meal is a force to be reckoned with but two foxes together on the same mission are a formidable duo who can resort to the most devious tactics to outwit the opposition.

Sat Nav knew full well the fierceness of the huge Herdi Goat and that he would have to use a every trick he had in his head if he was to distract Herdi enough to be able to snatch one of the young *kids*. The powers of his most sensitive nose had told him there were two adult goats close by the old cottage and two kid goats and the ploy he had arranged with Vicky Vixen was to attack from two sides on his signal which was to be a single *yelp*.

Rusty and Len had *grandstand* seats as they watched Sat Nav and Vicky take up their positions where they virtually crawled on all fours through the bracken, inches at a time, in order to spring their attack. The plan was for Vicky to dash in from one side to distract Herdi whereby Sat Nav would steal in from the opposite side and grab one of the young goats.

Mesmerised at the antics of the two crafty and stealthy foxes below, Rusty quietly spoke to Len. "I'm pleased it is not us they are after down there, we wouldn't stand a chance". Len was too spellbound to have even heard his brother's comments but something must have registered as he gave a shudder at the very thought of being caught by a killer fox.

"Listen to me Len" Rusty uttered sharply. "If we are to outwit any one of the Reynard family then we must study these tactics and learn from what we are witnessing down below" Rusty addressed his brother rather severely. It was Rusty who soon realised that, without the powerful gift of smell, the fox would not be so clever. He was watching the two deadly killers as they crawled ever closer and their noses were constantly sniffing which, again, reminded them both of the advice given to them by their favourite uncle, Big Bob Blacktail, 'If you can't see, use your nose' !

Sat Nav Nose and Vicky Vixen did not seem to be in any hurry as they inched their way closer towards their quarry and Herdi was becoming more agitated by the minute for his nose was not picking up the correct signals. This caused him to paw more frantically, digging up the earth in front of him as he did so and snorted even louder in frustration. The sudden sound of a yelp to his left caused him to focus his attention in that direction as Vicky Vixen dashed in from the right.

It was not the fierce Herdi who made the first move. Gerdi, mother of the two young goats, was first to spot the fast approaching fox and quickly challenged Vicky Vixen head on.

With her head bowed, Gerdi set herself to confront Vicky Vixen and she too snorted angrily which stopped the female fox dead in her tracks. Sat Nav Nose, on the other hand, used all his skill to distract Herdi as he menacingly approached the huge goat, more than three times bigger than Sat Nav, who was busy trying to tempt Herdi away from his family by using such bold and teasing tactics.

With his huge head bowed even lower, snorting and spitting, Herdi suddenly charged Sat Nav with such amazing speed that he was able to twist his mighty head and place his horns directly beneath the belly of the leaping fox.

In one swift movement of his neck, Herdi flung the attacking male fox high in the air and moved in quickly to finish off the old fox who had landed in a clump of dried and prickly brambles.

Sat Nav quickly realised he had taken on too much and that the huge goat was too strong and clever for him. He just managed to scramble from the brambles, tearing out large clumps of fur as he did so, leapt onto the garden wall and streaked away up the sheep track with the snorting Herdi close behind him.

Back in the old garden, Vicky Vixen was so intent on outwitting Gerdi she had failed to notice the defeat of her *admirer*, such was her intent to get her teeth into one of the young goats. Gerdi held the advantage as she had wedged her two frightened children tightly into the angle of the garden wall where she could easily fend off the attacking female fox.

Try as she might, Vicky Vixen could not penetrate the defences of the Mother goat. She skipped and jumped, yelped and barked, all to no avail as Gerdi's eyes, blazing in defiance, was trying to tell the fox that unless she backed off then she would have no choice but to attack and that surely would prove fatal for the desperately hungry and frustrated Vicky Vixen.

Bold and hungry as she was, Vicky, just like Sat Nav, had realised that she was not going to get the better of Gerdi Goat and suddenly found that she was now on her own and could hear the anguished yelps of her foxy admirer as he bounded up the side of Alnwick moor, hotly pursued by the ferocious Herdi Goat.

In a flash, Vicky turned tail as she too leapt over the old garden wall and streaked away southwards, her mind was already working overtime on just how she was going to find some food for her two hungry cubs, not to mention her own empty stomach.

From their grandstand view up on the chimney stack, Rusty and his brother had thoroughly enjoyed the scene down below.

"That was the 'bestest' battle I've ever seen" exclaimed Rusty.

" 'Bestest' asked Len. "Wherever did you learn such a ridiculous word" ?

" It's not ridiculous" answered Rusty. "I heard it on that mystery box in Sonny's bedroom and it means better than best, so there" !!

"Never mind, this is the 'bestest' chance we'll ever have to escape so let's get going" remarked Rusty as they scampered down to the ground below.

Rusty had already made a mental note of the best route to take while the skirmish was taking place down below as they set off at speed down a well worn sheep path where, only half an hour ago, Sat Nav Nose had passed on his way to court Vicky Vixen,

The strong scent of the crafty old fox was still evident in the noses of the two Redcoat brothers as they sped downhill on what they hoped would be the last lap of their journey home but, they were not to know what further troubles still lay ahead !

'Sat Nav nose'

Chapter Eleven

MORE PROBLEMS FOR DUKE REDCOAT

Rusty's disappearance from the Recoat family home had been the main topic of conversation in the woodlands around Alnwick for several months now however, the major topic of interest locally was the construction of a giant tree house just to the east of the Castle.

Every wild creature for miles around, four legged and feathered, was curious as to why the human Duchess should want to build another magnificent home when she already had the most fantastic Castle to live in, at least this was the gist of rumour and gossip which could be heard daily at the wildlife woodland café at the East Lodge.

Duke Redcoat, being the recognised master of tree house construction for miles around, found himself in great demand to answer the many questions as to the why, when and wherefore, was the human tree house being built at all ?

It must be said of course that Duchess Redcoat had more say in the construction of the red squirrel tree house but of course, ladies do not boast about such matters !

Anyway, Duke Redcoat's mind was often in turmoil because of the pressure from his immediate family to keep up the search for the long lost Rusty and his brother Len.

It had taken Duke Redcoat about three weeks to recover from the terrible wounds he had suffered at the claws of Buzz Buzzard when on his way, with his other son Len, to find Rusty and bring him safely home.

It was only when, early one morning, quite recently, facing a barrage of questions from all directions at the woodland wildlife café, Duke's attention was distracted by the mention of Rusty's name among a flock of chattering jackdaws way up in the top of a mighty beech tree.

Duke's ears strained to hear more, not really listening to any of the questions which were being fired at him from all directions. Two individuals in particular, Jack and Matt Jackdaw, were reporting the sighting of two red squirrels which they themselves had witnessed way over on the west side of Alnwick at the site of an old derelict stone cottage.

Duke Redcoat was beside himself with joy upon hearing this wonderful news but was careful not to show his excitement and pride which welled up inside him knowing that, if this gossip was really true then his two sons, Rusty and Len, were safe and well.

Duke also knew just how reliable were the jackdaw 'detectives' that he had no doubt whatsoever that what he had overheard was true.

With this comforting feeling, Duke took on board every conceivable question about the construction of the giant tree house and promised to investigate every one and provide the answers necessary to satisfy all concerned. This, of course, gave Duke immense pride, as it did his devoted wife Duchess Redcoat, who was always supportive of her illustrious husband.

Duke's daily visits to the tree house construction site always thrilled him and filled him with awe. He marvelled at the skills of these human builders but simply could not fathom out just why any human would want to live in a house up in the trees ?

After several such visits, Duke was entirely satisfied that this monster structure would pose no threat whatsoever to the wild creatures around Alnwick, on the contrary, many would benefit, especially the flying, feathered kind and, the sneaky long tailed kind of the Rotter Rat *brigade* come to that !

No way could Duke refrain from telling his dear wife Duchess about the news he had gleaned at the woodland wildlife café regarding their two sons Rusty and Len.

The crafty Duchess did not attempt to *steal her husband's thunder* and allowed Duke to impart what he had heard and she duly listened to his report. Of course, she was the most wise and intelligent wife of the leader of the red squirrel community and had, herself, overheard the self same chatter from Jack and Matt Jackdaw much earlier !

Now that Duke's mind had been put at ease, he busied himself with his daily duties and managed all his red squirrel council responsibilities while, in the meantime, Duchess took it upon herself to seek out her two, now grown up, daughters Milli and Yum, to tell them the wonderful news about their two brothers but, strangely, even they had not been seen locally for a day or two.

Duke's visits to the tree house construction site had now been curtailed because of the presence of two marauding Sparrow Hawks who had taken up residence nearby and were creating havoc among the population of small winged creatures.

None were safe from the constant attacks and the numbers killed or maimed by these two, low flying, *terrors* was alarming. At least this was the

'Duchess Jane Percy's fabulous tree house in The Alnwick Garden, It still exists'

information which had recently reached the woodland wildlife café.

Duke Redcoat had let it be known that he was indeed grateful to Jack and Matt Jackdaw for bringing back the great news about his two *missing* sons and now made regular trips to the woodland wildlife café each morning just in case there should be any further reports about Rusty and Len.

It was on such a trip for a quick snack of mixed nuts that Duke's attention was, once again, drawn to the excitable chatter among the jackdaw gang up high in the tree tops. The incessant *blether* was difficult to decipher so Duke had to get much closer to the chattering mob without spooking them in order to discover what all the commotion was about.

Duke made it as close as he dared but had to watch, and listen, intently to be able to translate the jackdaw babble and sign language where, again, it seemed to be centred around the intrepid jackdaw brothers, Jack and Matt who had apparently brought back some more news about squirrels.

Duke found it almost impossible to understand the exact gist of their story but it clearly did not involve either Rusty or Len, which was somewhat of a relief, as Duke considered that *no news was good news*!

However, what Duke did manage to translate was that; Jack and Matt had spotted a pair of squirrels many miles away, far over to the south east of

Alnwick but that these were not considered *normal* squirrels because these creatures were coloured GREY !!!

Now Duke Redcoat was a highly intelligent red squirrel and not prone to accepting any old gossip he heard in and around his woodland domain however, there was just a certain something about this tale which caused him to memorise every detail of the jackdaw rumour and file it away in his computer like brain for future reference.

He really was *positively positive* there was something about this story which caused his whiskers to twitch and, twitching whiskers were always an accurate alarm signal to any red squirrel, let alone Duke Redcoat, which could not, and would not, be ignored.

A troubled Duke Redcoat left the woodland wildlife café and made his way into the heart of the forest to the north where he could be safe and alone high up at the very top of an enormous redwood tree, a tree with the very odd name of Wellingtonian, a positive giant among trees.

This was always the same perch which Duke sought whenever there was some serious thinking to do. More like a *red squirrel office* really where he was completely alone with his private thoughts and knew he would not be interrupted.

'Grey squirrels' he pondered. "They must surely be very old red squirrels whose red coats have turned grey with age," thought Duke for this was the only logical conclusion he could reach.

"Why have I not seen old *grey* red squirrels before"? he asked himself. "My old Dad never did turn grey nor did my Grandad come to that ! This is all too baffling for me" thought Duke and promised to follow up on every scrap of information he could glean about these mysterious Grey squirrels and, he promptly fell asleep.

Poor Duke was no longer the agile *tree top traveller* he once was.

The horrific wounds caused by Buzz Buzzard recently had left him rather lame, especially in his hind legs which he relied on so much to leap through the air from branch to branch and tree to tree.

Duke of course realised that he could no longer rely on his speed of movement if he was to survive the many dangers and to escape from his attackers in future. He also realised that he would have to call upon all his reserves of awareness and intelligence to be able to stay alive because he was still the leader of the red squirrel community who relied on him so much for his leadership, advice and guidance in so many ways.

Never before in his six years, or was it seven, had the burden of responsibility weighed so heavily on his shoulders. The extra duties he had inherited involving the construction of the monster tree house were really sufficient to keep him fully occupied but it was now the additional mystery of the sighting of GREY squirrels, even though many miles away, was the matter which really tormented him most of all.

If only he could find out more about these strange creatures the less anxious he would be because, the fact that he did not know was worse than toothache to him not being able to fathom out such a mysterious problem and being unable to answer his questioners.

He was expected to be able to readily deal with any query put to him, such was the depth of his woodland knowledge and experience, but this GREY squirrel business was going to haunt him for some considerable time to come before he would soon learn of the terrible consequences which lay ahead for all red squirrels, **everywhere**.

'Duchess Redcoats family's Treehouse in an old woodland park.
It no longer exists'

Chapter Twelve

A WET AND 'DOGGED' PROBLEM !

Heading straight into the bright glare of the early morning sun, still low in the sky, made it difficult for the two Redcoat brothers to see clearly and Rusty was very much on edge because of this.

He was satisfied that they were travelling in the right direction because he had made a mental picture in his mind from the top of the old chimney stack while the battle between goats and foxes was taking place and, as on several previous occasions, he was going to use the never ending dry stone wall for cover until they reached it's end, then what, thought Rusty ?

Keeping close to the overhanging bracken for camouflage they made their way downhill until they could see the line of the dry stone *dyke* now clearly visible in the ultra bright morning sunlight.

Taking cover beneath the sandy coloured bracken, Rusty and Len decided to have a quick snack in the form of a hazel nut breakfast. This they managed by way of the two nuts they each carried in their cheek pouches, nuts they had saved from their early dawn visit to the hazel bush up in the old deserted garden.

Two hazel nuts were more than enough to *charge their batteries* in readiness for the hazardous journey ahead because each hazel nut is packed with an abundance of nutritious energy.

Fresh moorland water was everywhere following recent heavy rain and soon the two intrepid travellers were fed and watered and on their way once again.

Travelling downhill was less strenuous on their little legs and soon they reached the now familiar dry stone wall. It is called a dry stone wall because no cement is used in it's construction. The stones are cleverly bonded together without the use of mortar to form a strong structure, able to withstand the rigours of the extremely harsh winter weather on the wild, barren moors.

'Rainclouds forming up on the moor'

Two distinct warning notices made Rusty's incredibly sensitive whiskers twitch with alarm to tell him all was not well. First of all, a glance up towards the skyline above the wild moorland told Rusty to take notice of the darkening sky which had suddenly changed to a black and blue colour indicating that very heavy rain was falling from above and heading directly towards them as the bright morning sunlight faded behind the rain laden clouds.

This spelt immediate danger to the intrepid red squirrel as he racked his brains to think of a way to seek shelter from the oncoming storm.

The second alarm signal caused even greater concern to Rusty, and his brother Len, as both sets of whiskers quivered frantically at the sound of pounding horses hooves accompanied by the most terrifying sound of all, that being the barking and baying of the foxhound pack as they galloped towards them at an alarming rate, no doubt enjoying their early morning exercise.

Being down wind of the two advancing problems, Rusty was able to take instinctive action with Len close to his tail at the rear as they sped alongside the wall seeking any sign of refuge from both the torrential rain and the evil pack of marauding foxhounds. With the pack, and the storm, fast approaching, Rusty knew they had precious little time to escape unless they could find refuge close at hand.

Once again, *Lady Luck* played a big hand in saving their skins when they suddenly came upon a small moorland ditch which passed beneath the wall by way of an old earthenware pipe. The trickle of cold, fresh water passed below the wall at this point as Rusty led his brother into the mouth of the pipe to safety.

Half way through they managed to perch above the water level on a stone which had been washed into the culvert earlier and this, Rusty decided, was as far as they dare proceed. To move out to the other side would put both of them in mortal danger as the dogs would soon pick up their scent and attempt to track them down

These huge creatures could leap over the dry stone wall with ease so Rusty decided they would sit tight, at least for the time being.

Almost immediately the lead dog had picked up their scent with a nose equally as sensitive as that of any wild fox, or even better, as the snarling beast stuck it's nose inside the pipe.

The earthenware pipe acted like an amplifier as the sound of the killer dog's bark boomed inside the tunnel almost bursting their eardrums and Len was absolutely petrified with fear.

Rusty on the other hand was quite calm and collected because he had already recognised the fact that the pipe was too small for the dog to gain entry.

The volume of the din inside the pipe was soon coupled with the stench of the dog's foul breath which was enough to make the terrified Len physically sick as he quivered with fright.

The sound of the barking chorus from the rest of the pack was terrifying indeed even though most of the foxhounds did not know just what it was they were barking at. It was follow the leader at all costs and, if the leader barked, they all barked !

Some of the pack had crossed over the wall so now, from each end of the drain pipe, came the ear perforating din from the 'snouts' of two dogs and Len continued to shake with terror at the thought of being torn to pieces by such ferocious animals.

Then, at the sharp command from the dog handler, the pack moved on as quickly as they had arrived leaving the two, mightily relieved, red squirrel brothers to face the next impending danger which Rusty had already recognised.

Even though, with a foxhound sticking it's head into each end of the drainpipe shutting out the light, now they had gone, the darkness remained as the jet black rain clouds above swept down the side of the moor, unleashing a vast torrent of rain as it thundered directly towards the dry stone wall on it's way to the burn beyond.

The dreadful noise of the storm above was also amplified tenfold inside the drainpipe and, as a result, Len was unable to hear the instruction from his brother.

Just as Rusty was about to explore the situation outside, the vast cascade of flood water, deposited by the rain clouds, hit the top end of the drainpipe with such force it flushed the two intrepid red squirrels from the drainpipe with the power of a fireman's hose and they were rapidly jettisoned out through the pipe and continued on down the course of the moorland stream on it's way down to the nearby burn.

Along with all the debris washed down by the flood, Rusty and Len, bedraggled, battered and half drowned, were suddenly thrown up onto the bank side as the raging torrent suddenly changed direction, leaving them both soaked, shivering and all forlorn but nevertheless safe as the heavy raindrops continued to pound their bodies while the storm continued to rage overhead.

The thick black plumage had kept 'Corby' Crow reasonably dry during the storm, more than can be said for the two bedraggled Redcoat brothers as they lay on the edge of a patch of bracken, soaked to the skin.

'Corby' could not believe his luck as a possible tasty red squirrel meal lay just about twenty yards away, in fact two good helpings, as he spotted the two unfortunate and battered red creatures washed up on the edge of the ditch looking more like a couple of half drowned rats and he could not resist a pleasurable "Caw, Caw, Caw" at the sight of such a possible, delicious, meal.

The "Caw, Caw, Caw," shook Rusty Redcoat rigid at the sound of the huge, fearsome crow for he knew that the huge beak of the *fearful feathered fiend* could tear him limb from limb with no trouble at all and he prepared himself for immediate attack, or escape.

A quick silent kick brought his brother to his senses immediately as he followed Rusty into the dense bracken and, not for the first time in their young lives, the cover of bracken had come to their rescue.

'Rusty escaping from Corby Crow in the dense bracken'

The deluge of rain had now passed over and the bright morning sun lit up their cover beneath the bracken. Rusty was on extreme high alert because he knew full well the devious tactics of Mister 'Corby' Crow who had the advantage over the two red squirrels because he could monitor their movements from above the bracken. As the huge crow searched up above, Rusty and Len lay as still as they could although Len was shivering with cold, as well as fear, as he watched Rusty set himself on his haunches should 'Corby' Crow decide to attack.

From beneath the bracken, Rusty could clearly see the shadow of the evil, flying crow as it searched below for the slightest movement which would tell him exactly where his prey was hiding. Rusty was now in the crouched position as the dark shadow settled directly above them and Rusty knew they had been detected.

Timing his lunge to perfection, Rusty put every ounce of strength into his hind legs as he launched his lithe body upwards through the straggly bracken and struck the unguarded soft belly of Mr 'Corby' Crow.

With his two front, clawed, paws, plus his two incisor teeth, Rusty knew instantly he had made the perfect strike as he fell back into the bracken clutching two fists full, plus a mouth full, of black feathers. The awful taste of crow blood in his mouth told him he had inflicted a nasty wound on the surprised crow who by now had taken off skywards, wounded and embarrassed by the fact that he had been outsmarted by the fiercest of Red Squirrels, or, "could it have been a stoat ?" he wondered as he croaked in between his painful "Caw, Caw, Caws."

Rusty realised they must find a safe high place to dry out in the now warm sunshine but, more important, was the need to determine their exact location for surely they could not be too far from the safe haven of their own redcoat territory. Not too far away, Rusty's *telescopic* eyes spotted the top of a very tall Scotch Pine tree as it reached up into the sky and, with a sharp command for Len to follow, made a beeline for the tall, solitary, tree.

Rusty was amazed that he still had sufficient energy as he streaked towards the tree, hoping that Len would also make it safely.

What seemed to be an age, Rusty suddenly found himself at the foot of the enormous pine tree and, to his immense relief, Len soon arrived.

Together they climbed up to the very top to find the remains of an old, deserted Sparrow Hawk's nest where they rested up, secure at last as they stretched out in the mid-day sun to recover and dry out.

Len was soon in the *land of nod*, too exhausted to even utter a few words of thanks but Rusty's mind, forever active, was preparing the next, and hopefully, the final stage of their journey home.

Sunlight glistened on a large glass panel away to the north east which Rusty recognised from his journey back to the woodland park with Sonny all those months ago. Mightily relieved to know that he had charted their journey back home perfectly, Rusty was overjoyed at the thought of being back with his beloved family and friends once again but knew it would mean spending yet one more night at least, wherever, before they climbed the high stone wall which surrounded the wonderful woodland park which was their home.

Tiredness finally overcame Rusty as he stretched out alongside Len on top of the old nest and, as he at last relaxed, could not help wondering when he would be able to spend just one day without having to avoid the life threatening perils which had troubled him so much in his very young life so far. "Surely', he thought, 'there cannot be anymore dangers ahead to stop me reaching home safely" ??

Though extremely exhausted, Rusty's natural instincts prompted him to snip off enough small sprigs of pine needle twigs, sufficient to make a blanket to cover himself and his sleeping brother and at last, satisfied that they were also hidden from the preying eyes of any passing winged predator, Rusty joined Len in the *land of nod* !

Chapter Thirteen

DUKE REDCOAT'S DILEMMA

Duke Redcoat, leader of the Redcoat red squirrel community in the woodland park in Alnwick, had almost given up ever seeing his two sons Rusty and Len ever again, but not quite. His unstinted faith and belief in Rusty's ability to survive had kept him believing that Rusty and Len would eventually return home for he knew, according to recent reports of sightings of two red squirrels way over on Alnwick Moor, that they were still very much alive.

Duke also regretted having had to abandon his search for Rusty when the horrible attack by the evil Buzz Buzzard had almost killed him, which now seemed to be a very, very long time ago. It was so terribly painful for him to allow Len to carry on with the search alone knowing full well that he did not possess the same tenacity and resilience as himself, nor of his brother Rusty, yet, he would not allow negative thoughts to disturb him and longed for the day when they both would return safely home.

Being responsible for the welfare of the Alnwick *clan* of the Redcoat family weighed heavily on Duke's mind, especially now since the dreadful and mysterious deaths of two young red squirrels over on the far north side of the woodland park.

Two badly decomposed bodies had been discovered about one week ago by Victor Vole. Vic had been foraging, as is his main activity in life, when his acute sense of smell led him to the first corpse. Vic knew instantly there was something most evil connected with the death of this young red squirrel and, low and behold, only the very next day he discovered yet a second dead body of another red squirrel that he knew, without doubt, it was his woodland duty to bring this terribly sad news to the attention of the chief red squirrel, Duke Redcoat.

Vic Vole also knew this would entail an extremely long and hazardous journey for himself to reach the wildlife café on the other side of the park where he knew his discovery would be made known direct to Duke Redcoat.

Vic also knew that to embark on such a marathon journey could well prove impossible for his tiny legs to carry him all that way so he decided to *dream up* a scheme which would make life much easier for him and so, after his regular *siesta*, in other words, afternoon nap, a plan was firmly fixed inside his head which would save his little legs tremendously.

That very same night, Vic made his way to the track which led to a nearby cottage where he knew one of the woodsmen lived and also, that this particular woodsman left early each morning in his monster truck where he passed by the woodland café.

By the light of a bright moon, Vic Vole eventually arrived at the back of the cottage where the *monster* truck was parked and where, from the top of a pile of logs, it was easy to jump across and into the back of the vehicle. He soon made himself comfortable by tucking himself up inside an old coat and where he instantly fell fast asleep.

Vic's beauty sleep was soon disturbed by the ear shattering noise as the engine spluttered into life and rumbled out onto the woodland road leading eastwards towards the main entrance. After a reasonably short time, Vic ventured out into the open body of the truck and prepared himself to leave the truck at the precise time.

After a few more minutes the sound of the engine changed as the vehicle slowed almost to a halt before passing over the speed hump on the road which told Vic this was the journey's end for him. With an athletic leap, he jumped onto the tail board where he launched himself out into mid air and landed in the dense foliage on the grass verge at the side of the road without as much as a bruised *behind* !

Within minutes of Vic's arrival at the woodland wildlife café, home of Isobel and Oliver Grant, news of Vic's terrible discovery was being translated into several wild woodland languages which would soon reach the ears of Duke Redcoat himself. Enormously proud of his achievement, but not after taking his fill of a delicious breakfast of nut *crumbs* below the feeder table, did Vic scurry into the nearby sanctuary of the woodland floor, his mission complete.

Later that same morning found Duke also taking breakfast from the feeder table. He was now getting too old and infirm to go searching high up in the trees each day for pine cones and a *ready made* meal was simply marvellous for him on occasions such as this however, on this particular morning his breakfast was to be rudely interrupted when he overheard the shattering news of the two dead red squirrels which profoundly shook Duke Redcoat rigid.

His immediate thoughts were of Rusty and Len but was relieved to learn that, only earlier that very morning, news had also reached the woodland café that Rusty and Len had been spotted by two passing crows, way over on Alnwick Moor, alive and well. According to the two crows, they believed the two red squirrel brothers were heading in the direction of the Alnwick woodland park.

Duke's mind was in turmoil with the conflicting news but realised he had to act fast if he was to get to the bottom of the mysterious deaths of two red squirrels over on the other side of the park. His high intelligence told him that this was his main priority because it may well have a disastrous bearing on all other red squirrels in the immediate area.

Soon he was streaking, so painfully, northwards through the tree tops at amazing speed, belying his age and infirmity, such was the urgency which Duke rated the terrible news to be. He knew the exact location which had been accurately reported by none other than Vic Vole whom Duke had heard about somewhere on his travels a couple of months back..

Arriving at the scene of the first carcase, Duke, at a discreet distance, studied the body and everywhere else in close proximity to the dead red squirrel to record every minute detail in his photographic memory. Next, Duke conducted the same detailed examination at the site of the second dead red squirrel then, having taken in every scrap of visible evidence, headed for his favourite perch high up in a nearby giant Wellingtonian tree to *collect his thoughts*.

After deliberating for some considerable time, for Duke Redcoat was not one to hurry himself over such serious matters, having been taught by his very wise father that too much haste causes too many mistakes hence, he had managed to live to a ripe old age by being extremely sensible and cautious.

There was something very strange about the deaths of these two unfortunate red squirrels which puzzled and saddened Duke. They had not been attacked by a predator nor had they fallen from above as far as he could ascertain. There was absolutely no sign of violence nor even a playful game which meant only one thing to the wise old father and grandfather of the local red squirrel community. Well, one thing in three distinct categories, sickness, disease or poison. Which was it to be ?

Alone with his thoughts, Duke realised there were some things in life that he could not fathom out on his own and this serious problem needed a second opinion, and quickly, although deep down he believed he had just witnessed the first clear evidence of a mysterious deadly sickness but, he needed confirmation.

Concerning matters of great importance, Duke had always been taught that *two heads were better than one* and the only other head he needed to consult was that of his Scottish cousin, Big Bob Blacktail. Like Duke, Big Bob was a highly respected member of the red squirrel family. Duke's brain was constantly in tune but there was one very big problem, Big Bob lived up north of the border in Scotland !

'Duke Redcoat's cousin Big Bob Blacktail who lives up north in Scotland'

Always aware of the woodlands around him, and always on full alert, Duke's attention was drawn to a strange commotion in a tall beech tree nearby just moments before setting off on his urgent errand.

At first Duke thought this to be two red squirrels larking about but on closer scrutiny he was utterly shocked and demoralised to note that these were, indeed, not red squirrels but GREY.

Instant recognition of detail was sufficient proof to notify Duke that he was not seeing things for, in fact, these two alien squirrels did not have any ear tufts, as do all red squirrels and he knew he had just witnessed the horrifying sight of a deadly enemy which he vaguely recalled being described in a terrible tale being told to him by his great grandfather many years ago.

The seriousness of the matter in hand spurred Duke on and his first task was the stock up with *fuel* for the long and arduous journey ahead. Fuel was by way of a belly full of pine cone seeds to provide sufficient energy to make the return journey without any mishap and informing his wife Duchess of his plan, he was soon travelling northward in 'overdrive'.

No matter. All details of the horrible sighting were now firmly recorded to memory for future reference as he proceeded northwards, intently focussed solely on the arduous journey ahead.

The long trek took a little less than Duke had anticipated as he met up with his cousin, Big Bob Blacktail, just over the border into Scotland. This was most fortunate as Big Bob had only just decided to travel south in search of a fresh winter food supply for his large family and other local red relatives.

Duke did not delay in explaining the reason to contact his cousin and the two wise old members of the red squirrel *brigade* were soon in deep and serious discussion about the mysterious deaths of the two red squirrels in Duke's territory south of the Border.

Duke's decision to seek counsel with Big Bob had proved to be a very wise move indeed. During his travels around the Scottish borders recently, Big Bob had also heard disturbing stories of a problem in England whereby red squirrels were being infected by a deadly virus which was being transmitted by none other than an *alien* Grey squirrel. This tallied with what Duke had been told all those years ago.

According to what Big Bob had overheard, these grey creatures had been brought into England from over the great seas to the west long, long, ago and that they were the carriers of a lethal virus which kills the red squirrel shortly after they come in close contact with the saliva or urine of the grey species.

Big Bob had been intending to call on Duke to inform him about his suspicions and of this evil threat once he'd identified a winter food supply and was deeply upset when he heard the terrible news that indeed, the deadly squirrel virus was now only a few miles south and already seriously affecting red squirrel populations in the north of England.

Wise old Duke was pleased he'd made contact with his Scottish cousin, Big Bob Blacktail and, following their discussion, it was not difficult for Duke to recognise the extreme seriousness of the situation back home in the woodland park at Alnwick. The answer was plain and simple :- two dead red squirrels and two live grey squirrels, which he had personally witnessed, told him that this was the worst possible situation he had ever encountered in his long, illustrious, reign as Chief of the red squirrel community in and around Alnwick.

Big Bob further explained that, from his own experience because of his direct contacts with the large Scottish population of red squirrels, **there was no known similar deadly disease transmitted by the Scottish Grey species north of the border. Of that he was absolutely positive** as both the red and grey coexisted together in Scotland in harmony and good health.

All that was left for Duke to do was bid his farewell to Big Bob, partake in a quick meal of nourishing hazel nuts and retrace his steps southward as fast as his tired old limbs would carry him.

Keeping the afternoon sun on his right side, Duke's return journey back home was decidedly painful. Not only were his limbs aching but his mind was racing as he travelled on. Many terrible happenings in the wildlife park recently had disturbed Duke and Duchess Redcoat very deeply.

Not only the tragedy of losing their son Rusty, and then with added pain, Len who was now also missing, but a series of more recent events had given both Duke and Duchess Redcoat good reason for a great deal of concern. On top of all that, the extent of the recent destruction of much of their woodland habitat, plus most of their regular and well established feeding stations and nesting areas was also being destroyed which, in both their minds, was impossible for them to understand.

For the humans to come along and wantonly destroy certain sections of woodland, just to leave the debris lying on the ground, was in their eyes, wilful, senseless destruction. Furthermore, to have to cower high in the branches with fear when the many guns exploded to kill thousands of beautiful pheasants, their feathered companions of the wild woodland park so to speak, left them all in fear for their own lives in future. 'Why pheasants'? they all asked each other and *when will they point their evil guns at us* they asked themselves over and over again ???

Duke Redcoat decided he would soon declare a state of emergency, in his thoughts, as he journeyed south on his return journey. It was now foremost in his mind that he had to evacuate every red squirrel he could possibly contact from the woodland park which had been their home for countless hundreds of years and now, in only the space of a few months, their whole world was falling apart.

Duke had grown up to admire the intelligence of the human people, as had his forefathers, but now he detested, and doubted, everything about the most guilty of them for what he considered was their irresponsible and insane attitude towards their fellow living creatures. Such cruelty and selfish behaviour by the uncaring element of those responsible was beyond Duke and Duchess Redcoat's comprehension.

Getting ever closer to home, Duke's mind turned to his two lost sons. What if they had not returned before he led the whole red squirrel community out of the woodland park to safety. A message would of course be left at the woodland wildlife café but that might not be sufficient to save them should they accidently come into contact with the dreaded Greys !
Duke knew deep down in his heart that both his sons were safe and, according to information received, they were actually on their way back to Alnwick. The big question was; how long would it take them to get home?

Duke also knew they would be unaware of the frightful dangers awaiting them but his absolute faith in the two of them, especially Rusty, filled him with pride and confidence in the knowledge that, one day very soon, they would all be back together.

An extra problem was the fact that winter was *looming up* fast and speed of the evacuation was of the essence.

'Duchess Redcoat seeking information at the Wildlife Woodland Café.'

In the meantime, the dutiful Duchess Redcoat had made regular trips to the woodland wildlife cafe to glean every scrap of news which was filtering in from various parts of the wild and barren Alnwick moor.

Chapter Fourteen

THE MENACE BY MOONLIGHT

The cool evening air penetrated Rusty's bones as he awakened from a restful sleep while Len slept on in a virtual *coma*. Rusty wondered if there was another creature on the planet who could sleep as often, and deeply, as his brother !

'First things first' thought Rusty as he quickly gathered four large, ripe pine cones, one of which he carefully placed close to Len's nose. Twitching whiskers told Rusty that his brother was dreaming of a delightful meal, still too tired to wake up, and it took a sharp alarm call from Rusty, directly into Len's ear, to arouse him from his stupor.

A three-quarter moon climbed slowly over the North Sea as the two red squirrel brothers were enjoying a pine seed supper. Stripping the husks from the cone to get at each seed came naturally to the Redcoat brothers, being an inborn skill, and soon they were stuffed full of energy and now badly in need of a drink of water.

The first sign of the moon appearing in the east had given Rusty a very positive idea which was to continue on the next stage of their journey by moonlight.

Having taken in every detail of the journey ahead from his high vantage point, Rusty had formed a plan in his mind. The only snag would be if clouds appeared to blot out the light of the moon whereby he would have to find a suitable place to *hole up* for safety.

Not wanting to divulge his entire plan to Len in case a change was needed, Rusty instructed his brother to keep a close distance behind him at all times and not to utter even the slightest whisper.

After a final scan of the moor, resembling a *lunar landscape* in the moonlight, Rusty set off down the big pine tree at such breakneck speed that Len was already left behind, much to his brother's annoyance, and an early scolding from Rusty brought him on full alert.

They had soon quenched their thirst and Rusty quickly picked out a well used sheep track which ran parallel to the dry stone wall. Rusty's intention was to make for high ground where he could take his bearings from land marks silhouetted against the moonlit skyline as well as a few prominent lights which now glowed in the evening gloom.

They made steady progress along the smooth sheep track which pleased Rusty as he realised that total silence was of the utmost importance. The thought of an all night journey was frightening to say the least because they'd only had a previous brief experience a few nights ago when they made it in the dark to the sheep pen up on the side of the moor.

Suddenly they came out of the shadow at the end of the wall and were now illuminated in bright moonlight. As Rusty turned around he was shocked to see the white breast and *underbelly* of his brother *glowing like a brilliant beacon*. Big problem number one ! Rusty knew this had to be dealt with immediately and, just as soon as he heard the faint sound of running water, he signalled for Len to follow closely.

The little moorland stream trickled across the sheep path and Rusty did not relish the thought of having to plunge into the ice cold water but, what must be, must be !

Stealthily, Rusty took a deep breath and slowly slid into the water and out the other side to immediately slide his chest and belly along the muddy sheep track.

Len had observed his brother's actions but it took a brusque "tck, tck, tck" from Rusty to *gee* Len up to do the same and thus the problem was eliminated.

Much happier now that the matter had been resolved, Rusty knew if they kept to a steady trot they would soon dry out and warm up by getting the blood to circulate through their bodies as he led the way forward in a much happier frame of mind.

It has to be understood that most of the hazards and extreme dangers for many creatures in the world of nature's wildlife do not only occur during the day.

Small nocturnal creatures are always at risk from equally nocturnal predators during the hours of darkness and the reader must also be aware that a wild Red Squirrel is not a nocturnal creature.

Most creatures of the night have extra senses and a form of infrared vision to allow them to forage in the dark and also senses to warn them of imminent danger but, to our two intrepid Red Squirrel brothers, survival during this night time journey would depend solely on a high level of mental awareness every second, plus a huge amount of luck, if they were going to survive until morning.

Rusty Redcoat found it necessary to break his own golden rule of silence by having to harshly remind Len, again, to stay on high Red alert at all times.

Nocturnal predators, winged or otherwise, rely on stealth, silence and surprise as the three main tactics by which to capture their prey. Be it owls or foxes, both species have the same built-in instincts but, don't be confused with '*Orny*' the Tawny Owl and Barny the Barn Owl. Both are expert silent killers but only one is mainly nocturnal and that is Barny.

The Tawny owl parents will hunt mainly by day or sometimes at night depending on how hungry their chicks are.

The Barn Owl is strangely coloured creamy white, or even pure white in some cases, and can easily be spotted in the dark of night and one might think this puts the barn owl at a disadvantage when hunting yet, and even more strangely, this is not so.

The very design and structure of the owl's feathers, any owl in fact, are such that they can fly and manoeuvre in the air and also hover in total silence thus giving them a distinct advantage over their unsuspecting prey below and by which our two inexperienced Red squirrels were about to discover.

To call them inexperienced is just so in that they are not, in any way, creatures of the night.

Their lives are normally spent during daylight hours, high in the treetops or else on the woodland floor, where they are perpetually in overdrive. Their energetic and high speed existence is their normal way of life during daylight hours, hence they burn up so much energy that the hours of darkness are spent recovering their energies in a deep sleep in some safe resting place, way up in the trees.

To be loping along a sheep track in a large expanse of open moorland, on a moonlight evening, is totally alien to our two Red Squirrel brother's natural way of life but Rusty was positive they were making good progress and travelling in the right direction but totally unaware that their presence had not gone un-noticed.

Almost half a mile away, sitting motionless atop an old dead tree, sat the very menacing Barny Barn Owl, who, with his extraordinary infra-red night vision had spotted two distinct moving objects travelling way up on the side of the moor.

It was with this powerful infra-red, night vision, capability that Barny was able to detect two moving faint red glows which told him that two warm blooded creatures were on the move northwards, totally unprotected, and unaware that their presence had been registered in his radar like brain.

Barny, for all his long life's experience, was unable to immediately identify his probable evening meal.

He simply did not recognise all the signs his brain was trying to tell him so he could set his normal plan of attack which frustrated him terribly.

The images he had detected were not familiar at all which simply meant that Barny had to take a closer look !

The moon illuminated the open expanse of moorland and Rusty could focus clearly in all directions which was very comforting for him as they travelled northwards, and ever onwards, along the sheep track.

Twice they were forced to skirt around a black faced sheep resting up on the track causing them to struggle through the dense bracken in order to continue on their journey.

Meanwhile, Barny the Barn Owl had moved closer to the two mysterious travelling creatures, taking up his usual sentry position on top of an old telegraph pole. He found it hard to believe that the two warm blooded creatures were actually Red Squirrels who were far away from their woodland habitat and, even more so, were in unfamiliar territory which was all to Barny's advantage.

It was only when the big old, hollow boned, Barn Owl decided to get even closer still, as he flew silently to another vantage point, did Rusty's keen eyesight detect a slight glint of Barny's movement in flight against the moonlit sky.

Instantly he dived beneath the bracken for cover but Len, not fully alert, ambled on, unaware of his brother's action, or of the perilous danger he had put himself in. It was only when he realised his brother Rusty was no longer with him that sheer panic set in.

Barny was intrigued to witness the disappearance of one of the Red squirrels, which made his plan of attack much simpler as he set himself to launch from above toward his solitary prey below.

Realising the dangerous situation instantly, Rusty broke cover at amazing speed and leapt forward to jump on Len's back and knock him clean off the sheep track and into the bracken.

Once off the track they moved deeper into the overgrown foliage where Rusty signalled Len to lie low and perfectly still.

Any movement below the dense bracken would surely be noticed by the big white *marauder* from above and that would prove fatal.

Barny hovered silently and ghost like, about six feet above ground, unable to see the infra-red images of his quarry anywhere below. So he carefully 'quartered' the area systematically so as not to miss the slightest red glow through his line of vision.

Unable to detect any sign of life below, Barny decided to rest up on yet another high vantage point because he knew this was going to become a long and patient game and, as far as patience was concerned, Barny the Barn Owl considered himself to be the master.

Barny was not altogether sure if there were any rabbit or badger holes in this particular area because, if so, his task would be almost impossible simply because he would not be able to go to ground to flush out either of the two red squirrels and so, the *waiting game* began.

The moon climbed higher into the night sky, the temperature dropped considerably as Rusty lay on his back in the deep bracken.

All four limbs were tense and ready to strike out at the first sign of attack from above and every ounce of his very being was finely tuned, finer than ever before in his young life because he knew just what a *life and death* situation he and his brother had found themselves in.

Twice Rusty observed a passing shadow as Barny's image was highlighted by the moonlight above as he patrolled the area in flight but to no avail, for he had lost track of his 'supper', if only temporarily.

Rusty on the other hand was now desperate to seek a safer place for he knew this was a deadly game of patience and one wrong move would give away their position. A slow movement of his tail was sufficient to tell Len to bide still as he inched stealthily forward towards the sheep track.

Slowly poking his head out from beneath the dense bracken, Rusty could see clearly in each direction and, low and behold, there was a huge boulder on the side of the track about twelve feet away

The boulder itself presented no positive protection but, what if there was a convenient hole below the boulder then that would be *just the ticket* ?

'Boulder by the side of the track in bright moonlight'

Somehow, Rusty had to devise a diversionary tactic to (a) allow him to investigate the possibility of a hole and (b) likewise to allow his brother Len to make if safely to the boulder without being caught by the ever hungry night owl.

Rusty was fully aware that any careless movement below the bracken would be easily spotted by the wily barn owl and he had to make his plan abundantly clear to Len so they could work in tandem to reach a safe haven successfully.

It was a bold, risky and dangerous ploy which Rusty adopted to confuse the evil predator. Sneaking below the bracken until he found a hole in the foliage above, Rusty leapt straight upwards through the bracken and, dropping down below, quickly proceeded to another break in the bracken canopy and repeated this same strange action.

This proved to be the perfect tactic to confuse Barny Barn Owl who soon gave up the chase and floated away in the, now, early morning mist, disappointed that he had failed miserably to catch even one of the red squirrels. One in particular, obviously the leader, had *out smarted* him in every way possible

Inch by inch, Rusty crawled on his belly along the shaded side of the track getting ever closer to the boulder and every nerve and muscle was as tight as a *fiddle string* as he moved cautiously forward.

Luck again played a big part in Rusty's fortunes when he managed to make it safely to the boulder without any mishap for it looked as if Nadger the Badger had, at sometime recently, attempted to dig out a sett, which is what a badger calls home.

Nadger had obviously hollowed out a sizeable hole beneath the huge boulder to create an underground home but now, more than sufficient to give shelter to two desperate red squirrels in fear of their lives.

Moving quickly to find his brother, concealed beneath the bracken, Rusty squeaked an all clear signal to Len and the intrepid pair were soon out of immediate danger, safely below the large boulder.

Rusty knew from his early days in captivity at the moorland croft belonging to Sonny's dad Kevan that Barn Owls hunt mainly at night and sleep through the day so it was only a matter of waiting patiently for sunrise when they would be able to continue on their journey homeward.

It wasn't too long before early morning sun rays lit up the space inside the gloomy cavern and Rusty was off on a brief patrol to check out the land around to see if it was safe to move on.

With no apparent signs of danger, he called to his brother to follow and off they went at a steady trot with the early morning sun on their right side which told Rusty that they were heading in the right direction, northwards.

At the risk of giving away their presence, Rusty knew he had to take his bearings from yet another high vantage point in order to plan the way ahead. A solitary rowan tree down hill to the right gave Rusty the perfect opportunity as he suddenly changed direction and moved swiftly downhill with Len struggling to keep up.

Once perched on the highest twigs, Rusty soon recognised the familiar landscape, in particular the wooded skyline with the *needle like tower* pointing upwards above the tree line on the horizon to the north.

It was while waiting for the sun to show its fiery face that Rusty had come to the conclusion, for whatever reasons, that it would be better, and safer, for the two of them to separate once in sight of their final destination.

Len was not too pleased, if not a little afraid, when Rusty explained this to him but, once he realised that this was very much in his own best interest, he listened most carefully to the instructions Rusty *spelled out* and directed him from their high vantage point just exactly what he had to do.

Rusty even repeated his instructions three times for Len's benefit. He even allowed his brother plenty time to visualise and memorise the route he had set for him.

Just as they were about to go to ground, a pair of jet black crows lighted in the rowan tree but took off immediately they'd spotted the two red coated occupants. Bright red of course in the early morning sun which transforms a red squirrel's coat from a dull rusty colour in shade to a sparkling red in sunlight.

The pair of startled crows made a bee line north in flight for they had great news to carry back to the woodland park which they knew would be well received by all the interested creatures in the area.

The two red squirrel brothers said their fond farewells to each other with a brotherly embrace and moved on, each in a separate direction but Len, for whatever reason, had a very heavy heart.

Rusty also felt really bad about parting from his brother but he was more aware than Len of the increased dangers as they approached the end of their journey inasmuch as the risk of meeting stray dogs or some thoughtless youth with an air rifle who would not hesitate to pull the trigger if he got them in his sights.

Rusty had chosen the more direct and less perilous route for his brother and was confident he would make it safely home if he obeyed the instructions he had given him.

Rusty had elected to travel the more risky route along the backs of houses and allotment gardens which would undoubtedly present a host of unexpected dangers where he would require all his wisdom and guile to see him safely back home.

Unbeknown to either of the bold red squirrel brothers, certain changes had taken place back in the woodland park since they had been away, changes which had dramatically affected the very existence of all red squirrels locally.

These dramatic circumstances had caused old Duke Redcoat great anxiety and mental anguish for, not only had he possibly *lost* his two sons, or so he believed, but now he was faced with the enormous responsibility of having to care for all the remaining members of the red squirrel community whose very lives were now at risk because of a mysterious and deadly disease which had suddenly invaded their homeland.

The seriousness of this matter was more than Duke had ever faced in his long, illustrious, life to the extent that he had been compelled to seek further help and guidance from his blood relatives north of the border, in particular, his equally famous cousin, Big Bob Blacktail, who dwelt north of the border in Scotland.

Chapter Fifteen

'DECISIONS – DECISIONS'

Moments after seeing Len on his own way back to their woodland habitat, Rusty was inwardly disturbed. Disturbed at the thought of Len having to make his way alone on almost the last lap of their journey simply because, deep down, Rusty realised that although Len may well be able to look after himself up in the tree tops, he was not familiar with the strange and dangerous conditions which prevailed outside the woodland park at ground level.

While sitting on top of the huge boulder, Rusty believed, belatedly, he had made the wrong decision, the decision to split with Len, and this weighed heavily on his conscience. "What if this" or "What if that" were questions *twirling around* in his brain because he knew if anything happened to his brother which prevented him returning home safely then he would have to live with the consequences for the rest of his days.

"I won't be able to live with that" thought Rusty and his brain was in turmoil trying to arrive at a meaningful decision. "He is my brother but nevertheless, I am responsible for him and we have managed to negotiate many obstacles together so far, and now so near to home".

It was the sound of a frightening, blood chilling, scream which the early morning east wind brought to Rusty's ears. Rusty had already leapt from the boulder like lightening before the scream ended as he headed in the direction from whence the scream had come. There was no second scream which immediately registered in Rusty's brain that this was deadly serious because the scream had come from none other than his brother Len himself.

Focussed entirely on a fixed direction, Rusty knew that speed was of the essence and, as he travelled, several horrible, negative, thoughts passed through his mind because a scream of that nature meant only one thing to Rusty and that was *a matter of life and death*.

Bounding over the clumps of bracken and heather like a Springer Spaniel, Rusty soon found himself on the track he had, only moments before, directed Len to take northwards, skidding on the damp muddy surface as he picked up speed.

Only a matter of thirty yards on Rusty spotted Len's tail protruding from the bracken on the side of the track and he slid to an abrupt halt. Len's body lay motionless inside the narrow tunnel in the bracken and it took Rusty only two seconds to realise what had in fact happened to his brother.

Rusty got to work immediately to attempt to remove the deadly wire snare from around Len's neck. He managed to force his two front paws beneath the wire and release the pressure on Len's throat and eventually pull him free of the evil contraption. Even though the wire snare had been removed from around Len's neck he lay deathly still on the side of the path as Rusty got to work.

He quickly turned Len on his back and began to rapidly beat him on the chest with his front paws. "Come on Len, come on Len" Rusty shouted at his brother as he continued to bombard him with a furious flurry of punches.

Suddenly, Len's body twitched violently, then came a choking cough, followed by a sickening splutter as Rusty let up on the *beating* and began to vigorously massage his brother's chest and neck.

Rusty was mightily relieved to notice Len's chest begin to heave as he took in great gasps of air into his lungs. He then pulled Len over into the crouched position and rubbed his back briskly until he was satisfied that Len was, at last, breathing freely.

Fortunately, Len had been trapped in the deadly snare with his fore paws beneath his chin which had prevented his neck from being broken.

It so happened that Len had received an instinctive alarm signal, a warning of danger ahead, when moving along the track at full speed. He took what he thought was a safe move and dived into a rabbit tunnel beneath the bracken, unaware that a local poacher, or even a rogue gamekeeper, had placed the lethal wire snare at the entrance to the small tunnel in the undergrowth.

'Rusty rescuing Len from the poacher's snare'

As Len leapt for cover he was caught in full flight with his font paws tucked in beneath his chin. The wire noose had suddenly tightened around his throat choking off the air supply but still, Len had been able to expel every last drop of air in his lungs to let off the most alarming scream of his life. Only because his paws were also trapped beneath his chin was the reason Len was not now lying dead.

This particular type of evil wire trap is set in a loop with the loose end fastened to a stout peg driven into the ground. This primitive but lethal contraption is, sadly, still used widely by poachers, and others, across the land to catch rabbits but often other wild, and some domestic, creatures become entangled in the wire trap, almost always with fatal lingering and torturous consequences where a slow and painful death often results or, just as serious, a broken neck and instant death.

Luckily, Rusty had been at hand to rescue his brother who would surely have died had he not heard the piercing scream and dashed to save him and now Len, still lying on the ground, was busy soothing his sore neck by licking his front paws and carefully massaging his very painful throat and shoulder muscles.

From Len's breathless description of the alarm signal, Rusty believed, without doubt, that a pair of Grey partridge feeding up ahead on the track were *spooked* by Len's approach and had taken flight in fear, uttering their chattering alarm call, as they flew clear of any possible danger causing Len to take evasive action.

Rusty told Len that he had now changed his plan for the remainder of their journey homewards and that they would be travelling on together which worked wonders for Len's morale and the ability to recover from his traumatic experience.

Backtracking a little way to the large boulder, Rusty took a little time to reform the plan ahead clearly in his mind. They had managed to survive so far together despite the many dangers they had encountered on the way so now, with the woodland park in sight on the horizon, they would have to be more cautious than ever if they were to make it home safely. After all, he was surely entitled to make one wrong decision !!!

Nor was Rusty aware that their presence on the moor had been reported back to Duke and Duchess Redcoat by the two crows. Nor did they know that their father Duke had managed to survive his life threatening ordeal with Buzz Buzzard and return home also, and even more important, that their beautiful habitat back in the woodlands near Alnwick had been almost totally destroyed on instructions of the inconsiderate head gamekeeper and, even more serious, was the most alarming problem of the deadly virus brought about by the invading, alien, Grey squirrels, yet all this was not known to the two Redcoat brothers. Rusty's one and only desire was to negotiate the last part of their journey safely and successfully, unaware of the perils and pain which lay ahead.

Once again, Rusty was seeking out a high vantage point by which to survey the territory ahead. Looking skywards, he was concerned by the sight of dark, menacing rain clouds gathering to the north, once again, which meant that he needed to include shelter in his plan to negotiate the last lap of their journey and so together they set off northwards and on full Red alert.

Len had quickly recovered sufficiently from his ordeal to recognise familiar landmarks from his recent journey out with his father Duke. He mentioned to Rusty that there was a large post somewhere nearby which he had himself used to scan the moor ahead. This he recalled was close to a bare, sandy patch in the heather, riddled with rabbit holes, and to his sheer joy and delight he found himself on the very spot he had just described and was able to puff out his rather sore chest with pride that he had been correct as he saw his brother already perched on top of the very same post, scanning the countryside ahead.

Rusty knew immediately this was the same post used almost every night by Barny Barn Owl, and others, where they brought their prey to tear to pieces and devour. A cold, fearful shiver went through the whole of Rusty's body from nose to tip of tail at the thought of *being torn limb from limb* by either of these terrible predators. Furthermore, Buzz Buzzard, Gus Goshawk and 'Spooky'Sparrow Hawk will also use this post on occasions for the very same purpose.

At the foot of the post was a mound of dried bones and owl pellets which told Rusty that this old post had been used as a *butcher's bench* for many, many years.

Clearing the awful thoughts from his head, Rusty concentrated on the mission at hand as he carefully scanned the countryside to the north.

The dark, ominous rain clouds above Alnwick bothered him as they blanked out the mid-day sun. Home to Rusty seemed so very close and yet from his vantage point he knew that this *last lap* of their journey presented a great many dangers, especially now they were very close to a great many human homes and Rusty knew instinctively that this was going to be the most difficult and dangerous part of their return journey.

He could clearly see the fast moving vehicles travelling along the road, way over to the east but, top of his list of priorities was to find some clear water to quench the terrible thirst they were both experiencing. Food could wait a few more hours but now water was vitally necessary.

Both Rusty and Len had lost so much weight during their harrowing journey that both were virtually skin and bone. 'Not enough meat on me to give any predator a good meal' was the silly thought which passed through his mind but then he spotted a glint of water down in the valley where a stream appeared to meander northwards toward the woodland park.

Rusty was sure this was the Moor Burn which ran all the way across the moor and through the woodland park. Without anymore ado, he signalled Len to follow him closely as he leapt to ground and began to lope downwards on the old sheep path towards the stream. Rumbling bellies were audible as they moved on as neither brother had had a substantial meal for about two days yet they had exhausted so much energy that almost all their body fat reserves had been used up.

Rusty could just *smell* water as they got down in the bottom of the valley. The sheep track led directly to a clear, gravel pool which was sufficiently shallow to allow them the slake their thirst without having to overreach and risk falling in.

Just that short trip down into the valley had almost exhausted Rusty and Len was in a state of collapse such was their need of a good meal. It took Rusty almost every ounce of strength to climb a nearby tree but this was just for the purpose to confirm directions. With every joint trembling with fatigue, Rusty clung on desperately to some slender twigs as he scanned the countryside ahead and it was a wisp of grey, blue smoke which first caught his eye.

Grey, blue smoke meant a log fire and a log fire meant that kindly, country, people were most likely to live there and almost all kindly, country, folk always looked after the wild animals and birds by providing food. With all the required directions *logged* in his brain, Rusty estimated that they had three more hours at the most to reach food and shelter before the rain clouds *shed their very wet load* on Alnwick and the surrounding area.

Rusty did not need a second viewing but knew he would have to check again as they got closer to the little moorland cottage to make sure all was safe.

With the thought of a meal close at hand, this gave the two brothers greater incentive to increase their speed uphill but Len was now showing definite signs of weakness as he got further and further behind as the dark thunder clouds got lower and lower.

Rusty was forced to reduce his pace to a slow jog to allow Len to keep up, such was the weakened state of his brother which sorely worried him. If needs be, he would have to travel on alone, or else give him a *piggy back*, to seek enough food to *charge Len's batteries* but that would be a last resort.

Glancing up to the west, Rusty suddenly became even more alarmed to see a different cloud this time. This was definitely not rain. It was the *most feared cloud* of all, being that of dense smoke caused by a moorland fire, most probably the result of 'burning off' the heather by the landowner which seemed to have got out of control because of the strong westerly wind which had suddenly sprung up.

Rusty could even hear the crackling of the fire as the heather burned fiercely and the thick, dense, undergrowth which was actually being consumed at a rapid rate as the wild fire spread eastwards, directly down hill towards them. Unaware of the immediate seriousness of this danger, not having seen a moorland fire before, Rusty did not realise just how fast the fire was travelling downhill. A large clump of whin bushes in the path of the raging fire was consumed in seconds with flames reaching up into the sky.

The track had widened now to show two distinct tire tread marks, 'those of the game keeper's, or shepherd's, quad bike no doubt' thought Rusty as they ambled along. As if on cue, the *put, put, put* sound of the quad bike engine reached Rusty's ears. This did not cause him immediate alarm as they were now travelling through dense heather and all they had to do was sneak beneath the heather to avoid being detected and allow the game keeper, or whoever, and his quad bike to pass.

As the sound of the engine got closer, Rusty signalled Len to follow and led him along a small single track for a few yards which led to a feeder trough, a long wooden contraption which the hill shepherd fills daily with grain to feed his sheep on the moor when there is not sufficient grass to keep their *bellies* full. Only about nine inches high, this trough was ideal for the two travelling brothers to hide behind as the noisy motor loomed up before them.

The natural red squirrel curiosity got the better of Rusty as he stood on his hind legs, with fore paws on the edge of the trough, to see just who was the driver of the, now deafening, noisy quad bike. As it passed a gap in the heather, Rusty took a sharp intake of breath in astonishment as he instantly recognised the image of Sonny.

Even though he was dressed in heavy outdoor clothing, Rusty knew without a *shadow of doubt* that it was Sonny, the boy who had rescued him from certain death and looked after him so well at his human home so long ago.

The moment Rusty had looked at Sonny, Sonny had glanced to his left at the movement behind the feeder trough, as any smart country boy would instinctively do. He also beamed with delight when he recognised his long lost pet Rusty Redcoat peering over the top of the trough. The recognition was likewise instantaneous which caused him to stamp on the footbrake so quickly that he *stalled* the engine immediately which brought the machine to a sudden halt.

Len was cowering behind the feeder trough with fear and was amazed to see his brother openly displaying himself to this human with the evil machine and showing no alarm or fear whatsoever.

'Sonny on his quad bike'

At first, Rusty was somewhat reluctant to approach Sonny, and the thought of returning to captivity again flashed through his mind. However, Sonny's broad smile reassured Rusty who, straight away, leapt up over the trough and into Sonny's outstretched arms. Squeaking with sheer delight, Rusty was overcome with emotion as Sonny hugged and kissed him with so much love and joy having believed that he would never, ever, see Rusty alive again after all the many days he had mourned the loss of his dear, rusty coloured friend. Once again, the timing of their reunion could not have been more critical as the moorland fire raged rapidly down the hill side towards them.

All the while, Len looked on in complete astonishment at the amazing sight of his brother's strange behaviour with this young human but soon understood what it was all about. For this, surely, must be the young boy who had rescued Rusty from certain death so long ago and had looked after him so well.

A sudden cloud of grey smoke swirled down and threatened to suffocate them when Sonny called out to the other red squirrel to come quickly as they would soon be in terrible danger. Len stood transfixed with fear and Rusty jumped down and told Len that if he did not come with him and seek Sonny's protection then he would be *barbecued* in the flames within a few minutes. At that, Len followed his brother, rather reluctantly, up onto the quad bike.

Sonny gently placed the two trembling creatures into his inside pocket, started up the engine and roared away at great speed, away from the raging flames, to safety.

Rusty soon consoled his brother with comforting words as they sped along the track with the wind, and smoke, blowing inside Sonny's coat which immediately told Rusty they had just been rescued, yet again, from certain death. The hot air also told him just how close they were to the terrible fire and he wondered just what was going to happen next. One thing for sure, Rusty knew that Sonny had just saved their lives and now would do his very best to make sure that he and his brother would come to no further harm.

Len was absolutely petrified to be so close to a real live human person as he trembled inside the coat pocket. Rusty reassured his brother there was nothing to fear and that they had just been rescued from what would have been a horrible death in the burning heather.

The quad bike machine bounced over humps and hollows as Sonny raced on regardless to find a telephone to report the fire and soon, Rusty had

Len in a fit of giggles as they were jostled about amongst all the junk inside the pocket. Rusty was even bold enough to climb up on to Sonny's shoulder, just as he'd done so long ago when they were on the two wheeled bicycle together. Glancing back, Rusty gasped in astonishment at the sight of the raging fire as it swept downwards into the valley and huge clouds of dense smoke billowed eastwards.

Sonny was heading directly for the same cottage which Rusty had spotted earlier with the blue-grey smoke coming from the chimney. This is 'Whin Cottage' which belongs to Rose and Chris whose garden is another marvellous wild life haven and as good a feeding station as any to be found around Alnwick

The temptation was simply too much for Rusty as his stomach was aching for the want of food. As soon as Sonny pulled to a halt, Rusty called for Len to follow as he leapt from Sonny's shoulder and made straight for the nearest feeder box with Len hard on his heels. Soon they were gorging themselves on sun flower seeds, walnuts, almonds and peanuts from feeder boxes way up on the side of a silver birch tree.

What a *royal* feast with so many varieties of food to choose from..

Even though intent on satisfying the *pangs* of hunger, Rusty could now hear the strange wailing siren in the distance. Sonny's telephone call had alerted the Fire Brigade who were now heading for the moorland fire at breakneck speed. Both red squirrels were forced to cover their ears as the fire engine drew close to the cottage where the hideous sound of the siren was so loud, Rusty believed he would never be able to hear anything ever again while Len cringed with fear as the monster red truck, with bright flashing lights, passed close by the cottage on it's way to the raging fire.

The two red squirrel brothers had a grandstand view as the firemen directed powerful jets of water on to the raging flames and Rusty made a point of telling his brother just how perilously close they had come to being roasted alive only a few short moments ago.

Rusty was also quick to spot Sonny on the ground below, presumably telling Rose and Chris about the days when he had Rusty Redcoat as a pet. Having taken a good meal on board, Rusty warned Len to stay put as he clambered down the tree trunk *helter-skelter*, galloped across the garden and, in one bounding leap, he was once again perched on top of Sonny's shoulder, *nuzzling* in to his neck and cheek.

Such was the emotion that welled up inside him at being, once again, close to the boy who had saved his life previously. Sonny playfully tossed

Rusty high in the air repeatedly, catching him carefully, again and again, as Len looked on from above in utter amazement at the antics taking place before his very own eyes.

The sudden impulse for Rusty to be close to Sonny was unbelievably rewarding for the adventurous red squirrel and, by the looks of things, equally so for Sonny who was enjoying the experience immensely, especially in front of his friends, and neighbours, Rose and Chris.

Then, without warning, Rusty uttered a friendly farewell in the form of a stuttering chatter into Sonny's ear, bounded down to the ground and swiftly rejoined his bewildered brother up in the tree.

Len had stuffed his belly with goodies in the meantime and was dying for a drink of water but afraid to go to ground with three adult humans, plus the dogs, being entertained by red squirrels in their garden.

Rusty assured Len there was nothing to be afraid of and dared him to go get a drink. Len knew he could not stay up in the tree indefinitely as his stomach was simply bulging with undigested goodies and besides, after such a hefty meal, he was already thinking of having a nap.

Ever so slowly he made ready to climb down to ground level. It was not so much the humans of which he was afraid but he did not trust the dogs at all. He'd seen other dogs before in the woodland park chasing anything that moved and was extremely wary as Rusty coaxed him down from above. Finally he reached the ground and, inch by inch, crept towards the little garden pond keeping a *beady eye* on the dogs.

He finally had taken his fill of cool clear water and was making his way across the lawn when one of the dogs, Mac, could contain himself no longer. He set off towards Len in a flash, yapping loudly as he chased the terrified red squirrel across the garden. Len just made it to the silver birch in time as the frantic dog leapt up within a few inches behind him with *snapping jaws working overtime.*

Len's heart was beating rapidly as he scrambled to safety and Rusty, who had seen everything from above, was literally shaking with laughter at the terrified look on his brother's face.

"You told me it was safe" he chastised his brother. "That beast almost bit off my hind legs" Len cried. "He was only playing" Rusty tried to reassure his brother. "After all, we are trespassing in his garden."

"If that was play, I would not like to be in this garden when he's in a bad mood" retorted Len !

All three humans thought it was extremely funny but Len thought otherwise.

Sonny was now in serious conversation with Rose and Chris and Rusty would have loved to have been within earshot to hear just what the serious conversation was all about. *Decisions, decisions* again. Whether to move closer to them or to listen in or continue feasting and the hungry little *'gremlin' down inside his stomach won the argument* !

All of a sudden the quad bike started up and Sonny, having donned his goggles, zipped up his Barbour jacket and, before moving off, turned to look up into the tree where the two red squirrel brothers were munching away and waved goodbye as he *chugged* out onto the roadway before moving off under a great cloud of dust.

Rusty felt a tinge of sadness as Sonny drove away, especially when he had resisted the urge to climb down from above and bid Sonny goodbye yet again for what would have been the final time. Rusty was not to know at this time he would never set eyes on his dear friend and rescuer ever again.

The monster fire engine trundled up the moorland track on its way back to the main road, having extinguished the fire, to return to headquarters to await the next emergency call.

By now Len had taken his fill and was sound asleep in the cleft of a big branch where it joined the tree trunk. Rusty, ever mindful that they were not yet home, climbed to the top most twigs to reconnoitre the countryside around Whin Cottage.

His heart beat faster as he vaguely recognised familiar landmarks which told him they were almost home and that the end of a dramatic journey was almost over and, as he'd done on many occasions recently, memorised every sign in his mind to be precisely sure of every detail in order to complete the last lap of their journey.

The feeling of pride and excitement thrilled him enormously to know that, despite all the dangers along the way, the decisions he'd had to make had been correct. He also knew that, had he been on his own he'd probably have been back home much sooner but the traumatic experiences, so far, had only served to strengthen the brotherly bond between himself and his brother Len and that was paramount above all else.

To the north, Rusty could clearly see the high, grey stone, boundary wall which surrounded the woodland park and could not envisage any problems in completing the final lap of their journey.

Just as he was about to find a comfortable resting place to join his brother in dreamland, a stream of sunlight highlighted movement in a tall Scots Pine tree not too far away which instantly aroused every tense nerve, muscle, and even the whiskers on Rusty's chin.

The buzz he felt inside was like no other and, of all the decisions he'd had to make recently, this decision was the most direct and positive of all as he *skedaddled* down from the high point of the tree to awaken his *sleepy headed* brother.

The movement he'd seen in the craggy old Scots Pine tree was undoubtedly that of two red squirrels as the sunlight had illuminated their rusty red coats which shone like jewels in the late morning glow.

Len took some rousing as Rusty tried to shake him awake from his stupor and he had to resort to pulling a few whiskers to awaken Len fully.

"Come on Len" coaxed Rusty. "Follow me or else I will leave you behind" his brother commanded with much urgency in his voice.

'Len Redcoat fast asleep'

Len was down to ground level before Rusty but not in the normal way. In his drowsy state he had intended to follow Rusty's instruction and missed his footing as he attempted to climb down head first and suddenly found himself plummeting through the air as he fell all the way to ground !

As luck would have it once again, Chris had previously, and fortunately, built a compost heap at the foot of the Scots Pine tree and Len was extremely lucky to land on a pile of dry leaves and compost or else it would certainly have been the end of his miraculous journey back home with his brother. Rusty simply shook his head in astonishment as he witnessed the fall then streaked across the garden with Len trying his best to keep up.

There was a fierce determination in Rusty's every action as he travelled at breakneck speed downhill towards a small *stand* of pines. Sheep grazing contentedly in the nearby croft were *spooked* as the two red squirrels galloped straight among them on a direct *bee line* and, there was only one thought prominent in Rusty's mind and that was to meet up with the two 'special' red squirrels who were busy feeding on pinecones, just a short distance away, as soon as ever possible. Surely his red squirrel sixth sense could not be wrong !!!

Chapter Sixteen

A PLAN FOR THE BIG EVACUATION

Duke Redcoat had formed an elaborate plan in his head to evacuate every red squirrel from as far as he could organise throughout the woodlands surrounding Alnwick. This he knew to be vitally necessary if he was going to save the ancient red squirrel community from the dreaded mystery disease and, of course, this included his own Redcoat family.

Through the grapevine system of communication, which existed at the East Lodge wildlife café, Duke had let it be known that his message had to be broadcast as far as possible to reach out to the remotest regions. His message was that all red squirrels in the woodlands, everywhere, must gather at the East Lodge at dawn in three days time and, at all costs, they must avoid any contact whatsoever with their far distant, alien and diseased cousins, the Grey Squirrel.

All messengers were to emphasise this very fact that, to ignore this warning would, more than likely, cost them their lives. Furthermore, Duke Redcoat's message instructed all 'Reds' to eat as much nutritious food as possible beforehand to sustain them on the long and arduous journey northwards to Scotland.

Duke had spent several hours discussing his plan with his lifelong partner Duchess Redcoat who agreed totally with her husband. In fact, it was Duchess who had delivered his instructions to the wildlife café, making sure that all those who were well known for their gossip and 'the telling of tales' were informed, among them being Nutty Nuthatch, Matt and Jack Jackdaw also Mr 'Big Fella' Chief of the Cock Pheasants and a good many other tale tellers.

'Duke Redcoat (top) with Duchess Redcoat (below) feeding at ground level'

And so the plan was set.

Duchess reported back to her husband to let him know that his instructions were being instantly obeyed and the word was already spread far and wide.

Duke Redcoat felt the heavy burden of responsibility on his old, and aching, shoulders but moreover, it was the lack of any positive news about his two sons, Rusty and Len, which disturbed him most of all. It was absolutely imperative that they survived in order to carry on the ancient Redcoat *bloodline* for future generations of the Redcoat family and, for this very reason, he hoped and prayed that they would at least *get wind* of his urgent message. He, as with Duchess Redcoat, was also perturbed at the recent disappearance of their two daughters, Milli and Yum, who had not been seen locally for several days and poor old Duke Redcoat could only sit back now and await the awful day when he would have to lead all surviving red squirrels out of their age old habitat in the Alnwick woodland park to safety in Scotland.

This evacuation would have to go ahead regardless, whether or not all the members of his immediate family were present.

He was, nonetheless, fortunate that he had his dearest friend, and wife, of many years for comfort and who had borne him several *litters* of Redcoat offspring *in the good old days*. There were scarcely any red squirrels within many miles of the Alnwick woodland park who did not have Redcoat blood in them.

Duke was immensely proud of his position as head of the Redcoat Clan of red squirrels and, if they were to survive to continue the Redcoat *bloodline*, then there was no other alternative but to make sure that his plan to organise the mass migration of all reds to Scotland simply could not, and would not, fail.

Duke and Duchess Redcoat were rudely awakened early next morning by the all too familiar and dreadful din of the human *Beaters*. This told Duke that the killing season had begun yet again, as hordes of young men, rattling tin cans to make an awful din, were marauding through the thick undergrowth below, with the help of many gun dogs, to flush out hundreds of cock and hen pheasants from their regular roosting places.

This frightful practise is specifically used to cause the pheasants to take flight as they are driven forward in a particular direction where the human *killers*, all armed with lethal shotguns, are strategically placed, ready to *blow them out of the sky* and this caused Duke Redcoat to shudder at the very thought that so called intelligent, adult, humans could be so insanely eager to kill them *all in the name of sport* !!

How can they be called game keepers when they are really game killers ? !!!

The deafening salvo of shotgun fire continued at regular intervals throughout the day as the slaughter went on until there were no more pheasants left in that area.

Sadly, not all are killed outright, nor are all the birds which are *blown from the sky* found by the gundogs. Over the years, Duke Redcoat had witnessed this ritualistic slaughter from above where, for many days after the shoot, wounded and traumatised pheasant birds died in agony on the woodland floor where the shotgun pellets had left them seriously wounded or disabled. This rendered them incapable of finding a safe roosting place above ground level hence they are left to the mercy of the elements or else they finally fall victim, yet again, at the hands, or should I say jaws, of the prowling fox and other woodland predators or else, die a slow agonising death in the woodland undergrowth.

The agony of these poor, innocent, creatures which are not always killed outright goes unnoticed every year and the so called *intelligent* humans do not seem to care *one iota.* As if there was not enough death and destruction in the world of both human and wild life creatures without having to contend with the *lunatic* few who rejoice in the name of sport at the habitual slaughter of certain species instead of devoting their time and energy in the preservation of all wildlife species.

They appear to be so ignorant of nature's ways that they can allow an imported, alien, species of squirrel to spread it's deadly virus among the native red squirrel population yet kill off at random one of nature's most beautiful creatures, as with the cock pheasant for example, *for the fun of it.*

Duke Redcoat shook his head in sorrow and bewilderment as tears rolled down through his whiskers and fell like raindrops to the ground below. Now he was all the more determined to see his plan through to find a safer and more peaceful place for future generations of his Red Squirrel family and as many of their relatives as possible

This shooting may cause a slight disruption to his plan and may well delay their departure from the woodland park by another day but, hopefully, would give that little extra time for the whole of his immediate family to be re-united again in readiness for the long journey north.

Sightings of many more grey squirrels were being reported daily. This concerned Duke greatly for he knew that each day could well bring further tragedy to the red squirrel community.

He asked Duchess to check at regular intervals at the East Lodge wildlife café and keep him informed of the latest news and developments as he prepared to seek out some ripe pine cones as sustenance in readiness for the long journey ahead.

Duchess Redcoat had wisely added a further instruction to all the winged messengers which was to report on the location of any grey squirrels. This vital information would greatly assist her husband to plan the escape route into Scotland.

Duchess also knew, and feared above all else, that if only a single red squirrel of the assembled group became infected with the deadly grey squirrel virus then every one in the escape party would ultimately perish. Such is the intensity of this evil disease that Duchess was making two hourly visits to the East Lodge wildlife café to glean all incoming reports and pass on the information to her husband Duke.

The first report of a positive sighting of red squirrels came from several sources, mainly from the pheasant and partridge survivors of the terrible moorland fire recently. Details of early reports were sketchy at first but, as more and more information came to hand, Duchess found it difficult to control her emotions.

The story, as she learned, was the most incredulous of all in that several survivors had reported two red squirrels being miraculously rescued from the path of the raging moorland fire by a youth on a quad bike who just happened to be passing by at the time !

Further information of the same two red squirrels being sighted feeding in the garden at Whin Cottage established the fact for Duchess Redcoat that this could only be her two long lost sons, at least she hoped and prayed that this would be so. All this news she quickly passed on to her husband which acted like a magic potion and lifted his spirits enormously.

On the down side, the odd report was being received of the dreaded grey variety of squirrel but not near as many as Duchess Redcoat had anticipated.

All of a sudden Duke was his old *bossy* self again. He even felt a surcharge of energy which he believed he'd lost forever as he quickly gathered his wits about him and began putting the final touches to his elaborate evacuation plan in to his *data base*.

The wildlife *grapevine* in nature must be about the most efficient information gathering service anywhere on the planet. Soon the whole area adjacent to the East Lodge wildlife café was buzzing. Not with wild bees or wasps but with the sheer volume of wild creature chatter as the relevant information came in from far and wide. Every conceivable creature, winged, or four footed, was in someway involved to the extent that the *babble and chatter* was incessant.

Duke had now joined Duchess to help assimilate every snippet of information which was being brought to *base*. Duke was quick to discard any story he believed to be irrelevant as it only served to complicate matters but, all the while, a healthy pattern began to emerge which Duke knew, in his very old bones, was just what he had prayed for only a few short days ago.

More than that, he had been able to glean certain snippets of information himself about two distinct sightings of *two separate pairs* of red squirrels, not too far away to the south of the woodland park. These stories were just too good to be true he told himself as his brain was working at such a speed it caused him to become as *dizzy as a coot* !

No way would he impart this knowledge to Duchess just yet in case it was all a false alarm but, nevertheless, he really was now on a high whereas yesterday, he had just felt like giving up altogether.

Duke could hardly believe where he found the energy to climb to the very topmost twigs of the tallest tree in the woodland park, the giant Wellingtonian. Here he was able to contemplate in peace and quiet but, and just as important, to seek out the weather pattern for the next few days.

His many years experience in the wild had taught him to read the clouds in the sky and smell the wind. This natural skill had been passed down in his red squirrel genes from generation to generation and enabled Duke to register in his brain this valuable information and so be able to plan ahead accordingly. On this occasion, all the signs he'd seen, and *sniffed* out, appeared to be favourable.

Way up on the *roof* of the woodland park, Duke caught the occasional glimpse below of a red squirrel deliberately making a *beeline* towards the East Lodge, all the while searching out the precious food just as Duke had instructed in readiness for the mass exodus.

What Duke Redcoat could not see was the small copse of pine trees, less than a mile to the south of the woodland park where two female red squirrels were busy feeding on the delicious pine cones. Nor was he able to see the open meadow where two male red squirrels were heading at *breakneck speed* towards the same stand of pine trees where the two females were busy feeding.

Had he known, in fact, that these four red squirrels were his own flesh and blood, namely Milli, Len, Yum and Rusty Redcoat, his very own millennium family, then Duke Redcoat would probably have attempted several, celebratory, triple summersaults and most probably have fallen from the top of the monster Wellingtonian tree with shock !

The activities of these four red squirrels however, had not altogether gone unnoticed. Cushy and Woody Cushat, two thieving wood pigeons, were digesting the meal of winter cabbage they had just stolen from Chris and Rose's garden at Whin Cottage. Their crops were *full to the gunnels* as they sat up high at the top of a Sycamore tree where, despite their continuous *cooing*, a sure sign of Cushat contentment, they were about to witness one of the most significant happenings in the history of the Alnwick Redcoat squirrel family.

Both Woody and Cushy could sense the electrifying excitement building up between the two feeding female reds and the two, fast approaching, red males as they sped across the open meadow.

Aware of Duke Redcoat's urgent instruction to report all red squirrel sightings, both Woody and Cushy suddenly became most attentive, taking in every joyous movement and action leading up to the actual reunion. After all, there was a great deal of prestige at stake here.

To have spotted one red squirrel was a real feather in their caps but to report a sighting of *four* would elevate them to the very top in the pecking order of spies among all their wild feathered friends of the woodland park.

Their names would always be remembered as the two extra smart birds who witnessed the reunion of the young Redcoat family and they would be famous for evermore, ***or so they thought*** !!!

None present had taken any notice of Jack and Matt Jackdaw who had also, but more discreetly, witnessed the reunion celebration of the four young Redcoat children from their own vantage point and were now well on their way to the East Lodge wildlife cafe to *steal the thunder* from Woody and Cushy Cushat !!!

Chapter Seventeen

A JOYOUS REUNION

The enormous range and acute vision of any red squirrel is just what nature has provided as a means of defence. Defence against its' many enemies in the wild at tree top level as well as on the ground.

On this particular day however, it was not as a means of defence that this extraordinary gift of nature came into its' own.

From high in the pine tree, both Milli and Yum quickly spotted two red squirrels 'haring' across the open meadow. In turn, the two red squirrels, 'haring' across the open meadow had their eyes sharply focussed on the two red female squirrels up in the tall pine tree.

As well as being blessed with fantastic eyesight, red squirrels also have a built in E.S.P. (extraordinary sensory perception). For example; the unique gift of recognising the presence of another of it's own species at a distance, even without necessarily seeing one another.

The electronic 'vibes' charged each of the four red squirrels with an invisible surge of excitement knowing full well that the most joyous moment in their young lives to date was about to take place.

Both Milli and Yum stopped feeding and began a sequence of the most daring, dangerous and electrifying 'gymnastics', impossible to describe. More like a tree top ballet dance. Both had clearly now recognised that their two long lost, loving brothers, Rusty and Len, were heading for the large pine tree.

Rusty, with Len close on his heels, only had a few short yards to travel and a simple post and rail fence to negotiate then, it was up the trunk of the big old pine tree at 'full pelt'.

Squeaks, squeals and squawks of sheer joy and delight could now be heard all around the old pine tree as brothers and sisters of the Redcoat family entered into a remarkable frenzy of hugs, cuddles, leaps of joy and mad, carefree chases on the large pine branches at breakneck speed. At this the girls were, by far, the more superior having spent the last several months of their lives in the tree tops. The boys, on the other hand, had spent too much time at ground level and were mere novices by comparison.

United at last, this fantastic display of greeting, the sheer delight and elation of being together again, had all been recorded in the photographic memories of Woody and Cushy Cushat. Privileged, as they believed they were, to have been first to witness this rare tree top spectacular, the two proud 'Woodies' were now on their way back to report their 'headline' news to whoever happened to be at the East Lodge wildlife café.

Not one of the four young red squirrels had taken any notice of anything other than themselves. Such was the dramatic effect the emotional reunion was having on each of them.

Incessant, excitable chatter was now the order of the day as the celebratory antics continued high above ground. It was a case of who could outdo the other as each demonstration of agility became more elaborate and death defying and soon it was very obvious just who were the two fittest members of the Redcoat family.

Rusty made the excuse that he just wanted to talk and, of course, Len agreed wholeheartedly as they were both exhausted, for their long and arduous journey home had really taken its' toll on their general health.

Finally, the two Redcoat sisters wore themselves out and were only too pleased to sit close to their long lost brothers and listen to the fantastic stories and descriptive tales about their adventures away from the woodland park of their attempt to get safely back home.

So much to tell. One tale led to another and all the while Milli and Yum sat spellbound as one scary incident after another was told in detail, much to their pride and delight.

Even as they chatted, Rusty, still ever on high alert, was keeping a watchful eye on the dark, menacing rainclouds to the north. Milli, for her part, was building up sufficient courage to tell her brothers about the mysterious, and deadly disease which had taken the lives of at least two red squirrels recently but, for the present, she could *not get a word in edgeways.*

Milli could sense that Rusty was anxious to make the last part of their momentous journey back to the woodland park without further delay, especially to be able to greet his long lost parents, Duke and Duchess Redcoat

At long last Milli was now able to impart the terrible news about the mystery disease in the woodland park and to advise Rusty and Len that it would be much wiser, and sensible, if they all remained in the small stand of pine trees for the night ahead where they could 'feed a plenty' and have a good night's sleep before making the last mile of their journey home.

Although somewhat reluctant, Rusty agreed on two counts. One, he still had time to take on some much needed food and secondly, the dark rainclouds to the north looked very menacing indeed and there just happened to be plenty shelter exactly where they were.

Even though the two Redcoat sisters realised the need for their loving brothers to eat their fill, they could not resist asking one question after another, such was their curiosity. They had missed, terribly, the early weeks and months of their young lives since their treetop home was destroyed and were naturally anxious to learn all about those absent times.

It was not only the two 'crafty' Cushats who had witnessed the joyous reunion. Many other winged creatures had also been 'accidently' present to see the tree top celebrations including Jack and Matt Jackdaw for they too recognised the importance of this happening and wanted to be first to break the good news back home within the confines of the high stone wall surrounding the woodland park.

Not many birds can boast being more intelligent than the wily Jackdaw who had always been one step ahead of the rest and, by now, the whole of the wildlife community inside the park would have been made aware of the great news nevertheless, a great many little wings were beating as fast as they could to carry their glad tidings back to base as well., all wanting to be *in on the act*.

Rusty had already reckoned it would soon be dark, especially now that the rain laden clouds were beginning to gather directly above. Just on the edge of the copse stood a sturdy building built of oak. This very old rustic structure had been there for many years and it served as a shelter for livestock in bad weather as well as a feeding station during the winter months.

Locally it could well be called a 'hemmel' and was presently stocked with a dozen or so bales of hay and Rusty knew instinctively just where the young Redcoat family would be spending the night.

'The old Hemmel where the young Redcoat family took shelter'

The thunder storm broke directly above just as they'd all got settled, up in the old oak rafters inside the hemmel.

This was the opportunity Milli had been waiting for and was quick to get Rusty alone for a few moments to elaborate further about the terrible dangers in their local woodlands where the deadly 'bug' was causing the most horrible illness and certain death to red squirrels and, seemingly, for no apparent reason at all.

She also made sure that emphasis was made about the possible cause being blamed on their distant, but foreign, grey English cousin who, it is believed, are the carriers of the deadly virus. Milli went on to describe in detail the seriousness of living, or even just feeding, in their old woodland habitat and this was the very reason that she and Yum had been way outside the woodland park.

Rusty was also made aware of the urgent message Duke Redcoat had sent out to all red squirrels, locally, to gather at the East Lodge and that they must all congregate there tomorrow.

Down below in the hay other wild creatures had sought shelter under the same roof and Rusty knew full well that several members of the 'Rotter' Rat family were among them. The downpour was torrential but, not even the thunder and lightening would bother any of them as their earlier, hectic, activities had sapped each one of every gram of energy and soon, all four were huddled together up in the roof space, fast asleep.

The night was spent in perfect bliss and contentment. This was just as well really as none of the four Redcoat brothers or sisters had even the slightest inclination as to what the next two or three days was about to bring, for, once again, their family life was about to be seriously disrupted and changed forever.

A heavy morning dew created the perfect conditions for a long needed wash for each of the redcoat youngsters. An age old, moss covered, fallen pine tree nearby provided the ideal bathing facilities where each young squirrel was able to propel his or her body along the saturated, moss covered, tree trunk where every square centimetre of their rusty red and white coat was thoroughly cleaned.

This was a magical sight to behold in the early morning sunlight for, as with most red squirrel activities, they simply turned this necessary morning ablution into a hilarious game of who could slide the furthest distance along the log !

With fur coats sparkling, the four young 'reds' set about quenching their thirst and finding sufficient food to sustain them on the final mile back to the woodland park.

All four were soon perched together on the very top of the tallest pine tree where, together, they planned the journey home whilst having breakfast at the same time. The route ahead seemed straight forward but Rusty was not going to be easily led into a false sense of security as, from previous experience, he knew just what possible dangers could be lurking ahead.

With just the slightest squeak, Rusty led his siblings down to ground level as off they sped in a northerly direction across open meadow. Early morning always presented more challenges to almost all wild creatures than at any other time of the day and this day was no exception.

Chapter Eighteen

THE FATEFUL DAY

Dawn broke over the woodland park as peaceful as ever before. Duke Redcoat had been awake most of the night because the responsibility for what was about to happen weighed heavily on his mind.

As he sat atop his favourite, giant, Wellingtonian redwood tree for the very last time he deliberated on his plan to evacuate the whole red squirrel community from the Alnwick woodland park to safety in Scotland. This plan involved a terribly long trek northwards in order to escape the deadly sickness affecting his very ancient and noble Redcoat family line, transmitted by the alien Grey squirrel who is, unfortunately, the carrier if this deadly virus.

What hurt and concerned Duke Redcoat more than anything was the fact that human beings were the cause of this calamitous situation. Thinking aloud, Duke uttered, 'Why is it that humans can wantonly kill thousands of one of nature's most beautiful and innocent creatures, namely the Pheasant, yet allow the deadly, disease ridden, Grey squirrel to invade and create this death and destruction.? "THIS HAS TO BE WRONG" shouted Duke Redcoat in anger and despair at no one in particular but, knowing deep down that those who should be listening could not hear his cry and couldn't care less even if they could.

'How would they like to lose their mighty home and lands to some raiding marauder with no one to care *two hoots* about them'? were Duke's thoughts.

The very future of all red squirrels locally depended solely on Duke Redcoat now to successfully organise the mass exodus and so save as many of his own blood line as possible.

Duke knew his message had been widely received and he expected a large attendance at the East Lodge wildlife café later in the day but, on top of all his worries, was the fact that all four of his own immediate children could not, as yet, be accounted for. This troubled Duke sorely but, such was the importance and urgency of his mission, he knew that if the worst should turn out to be the very worst, then he would lead all the surviving 'reds' out of the woodland park to-morrow, with or without his own four children.

He had a positive, and bold, escape route already programmed into his own sat nav brain for the long, arduous, journey which he planned to start just before dawn to-morrow morning and which he knew would be far from easy.

Later this afternoon he would address all red squirrels present and instruct them severely on the importance of his plan and that all concerned must obey his every command implicitly, and without question.

The first, and longest, stage of the journey would take them right up to the mighty River Tweed. This would present them with the severest of all challenges, that being just how to cross the mighty wide expanse of the vast and fast flowing river.

Duke knew that once he had mastered this final stage of the journey then the remaining few miles into Scotland would be comparatively simple.

In recent days he had sat studying his local River Aln for hours on end, planning the safest way to cross then multiplying the *degree of difficulty* ten times, such was the enormity of the problem with the giant River Tweed.

Duke's train of thought was disturbed by the distant *hub-bub* of excitable twitter and chatter coming from the direction of the East Lodge. Not wanting to lose his concentration on the matter in hand, Duke resisted temptation to hurry straight over to see just what all the fuss was about when, as if on cue, Jack and Matt Jackdaw glided silently in towards the giant Wellingtonian tree and settled on a branch directly below where Duke was perched.

They had already broken the great news of the four *missing* Redcoat youngsters to the large gathering over at the East Lodge but, when they learned that Duke was close by in his favourite tree, they did not waste a second just in case he heard the terrific news from other *beaks*. Woody and Cushy Cushat for instance !!!

'*The giant Wellington trees towering into the sky, where Duke Redcoat sought privacy in order to do his thinking and planning*'

Duke was *soaking up* the last nostalgic scenes of his woodland home when he distinctly heard the approach call of his beloved Duchess. She knew full well just how much he would need her support on this sad, sad day as she hurried through the treetops to be by his side. No sooner had she taken her place beside him up at the top of the giant tree when, from down below, Jack and Matt Jackdaw decided to impart their fantastic news directly to the parents of the four missing red squirrels.

In their chattering tones, they let Duke and Duchess Redcoat know every detail of the sighting of their four young siblings less than a mile to the south of the woodland park. They expressed in elaborate detail the *harem-scarem* celebratory antics of the four red youngsters as they finally met up with each other in the old Scot's pine tree just over by Whin Cottage about one mile away on Alnwick Moor.

Duchess was beside herself with absolute joy when she heard the wonderful news, so much so that Duke could hear her heart beating wildly in her chest with relief and excitement of such glad tidings and they both hugged and held each other in a long and loving embrace, speechless, but totally overcome with the emotional joy of it all.

Through all the long absence of young Rusty, then the loss of Len, Duke had managed to survive the most terrible ordeal out on the wild moor yet, once he'd managed to return home, seldom did he doubt that his two sons would eventually return safely. Well ! maybe just once, or even twice !!! To this end he never stopped convincing Duchess that this would be so but, for their return to have coincided with the most traumatic and important time in the history of the Redcoat family, it was all the more reason why neither Duke nor Duchess Redcoat could stop the tears of emotion as they shared this wondrous time together.

For Duke, this was the best ever omen he could have wished for and his strength and resolve to deal with the emergency in hand was boosted beyond words for, and above all else, Duke was now more convinced than ever before that his plan to save the whole local red squirrel community could not, and would not, fail.

With one final look from their lofted perch, Duke and Duchess Redcoat absorbed every last detail of their beloved home land before moving off to the woodland wildlife café at the East Lodge to join the ever increasing numbers of red squirrels gathering, as instructed, to await final instructions from their Chief about their final departure.

After thanking Jack and Matt for their wonderful news, Duke Redcoat led Duchess on a zig-zag trip back to the East Lodge, trying to say farewell to as many of his favourite trees as possible on their final journey through the woodland park. As they travelled, each allowed so many fond memories to pass through their minds, memories of such marvellous, peaceful, blissful times of their lives in the park.

This only served to increase the pain to an almost unbearable level but, at least, they could now look forward to a long awaited, joyous, reunion with their two long lost sons as a form of compensation.

In all his long life in the woodland park, Duke Redcoat had never, ever, witnessed such a massive gathering of so many wild, woodland creatures now assembled at the East Lodge.

Vast numbers of birds of all descriptions were assembled in the trees, as well as many four footed creatures at ground level who had come to bid their own farewell to their red squirrel friends.

The volume of so much *twitter, chitter, chatter, chirping, squeaks and squawks* was deafening. Suddenly it increased to a roar as news reached the throng via Woody and Cushy Cushat, rather belatedly as it happened, that four young red squirrels had been spotted less than a mile away and were now heading north towards the assembled horde.

Once again, Duke and Duchess were overcome with emotion at such a huge turnout from their fellow wild creatures. Duke had decided to take a back seat in order to keep his composure, fully aware of the responsibility he had taken on board and not wanting to be distracted in the slightest.

More and more winged creatures were joining the throng and, with every new *winged* arrival, came a fresh progress report on the four young red squirrels as they also made their very last lap of their journey homeward.

Quite suddenly, Duke Redcoat became aware of the presence of *Orny* the Tawny Owl who had silently, almost *ghost* like in fact, taken up a position close beside him. *Orny's* presence unnerved Duke at first, having such a silent *predator* so close by his side but, for some strange reason, Duke did not even *flinch*. The reassuring hooting tone of the wise old owl told Duke to pay attention to what *Orny* was trying to impart.

"All will be well" said *Orny* to Duke " Do not despair. You must look carefully for the vital clue which will be the solution to your immediate problem" and, with that simple but dramatic statement, *Orny* finally uttered "Farewell my fine and trusted woodland friend" as he gracefully took wing and glided like a silent shadow out of sight in the dense foliage below.

Knowing for years the wisdom of *Orny* the Tawny Owl, Duke knew he had to be most vigilant if he was to solve the *riddle* of *Orny's* farewell message. This advice was most valued and Duke knew instinctively that he would not get a second chance to identify the clue to which *Orny* had referred to and presented him with.

It was now time to concentrate on the immediate task of getting all the red squirrels together. It did old Duke Redcoat's heart good to see so many red bushy tails visibly evident all around. Not able to count the numbers exactly, he estimated about seventy, or more, were present, far more than he'd ever believed existed so close to his woodland territory.

Duchess meanwhile had taken up her sentinel position on the highest twig above the East Lodge in anticipation of the arrival of her four young, millennium siblings. Her heart was *swollen* with motherly pride and devotion having had to suffer months of pain and anguish at the loss of her two sons which was now about to end.

She was deliriously happy and content in the thought that they would now be all together in the departure from their ancestral home and the adventure which was about to take place to seek a safe new home somewhere in the north.

The sudden appearance of a huge cattle truck caused much dismay among the wildlife gathering as it attempted to pass below the archway at the East Lodge entrance. Almost all present fully expected the truck to be far too high to negotiate the arch as they looked down in *awe* yet, with only a few inches to spare, the big wagon slowly passed through the archway and continued on it's journey into the park with it's consignment of six *shaggy, rusty red coated*, Highland cattle.

Chapter Nineteen

YET MORE CHALLENGES

All four young red squirrels knew instinctively that breakfast for them was a relatively simple chore but for some others in the wild, it meant capturing and killing their prey in order to satisfy their appetite and, for this very reason, four pairs of eyes, and ears, were strained to the limit for the slightest signs, or sounds, of danger.

Rusty took charge automatically as he led the way. His plan was to pick up the Moor Burn trail which, apart from having plenty safe cover, journeyed on northwards and ultimately passed through the woodland park to end it's journey in the River Aln.

They made good progress as they travelled down hill among the placid sheep, already grazing. This pleased Rusty because sheep automatically lift their heads at the slightest concern around them and this advance warning would prove vitally important to the travelling quartet before the morning was out.

Buzz Buzzard and three of his family, or friends, were soaring high on the wing up above and all four *wee reds* knew they would not be travelling unnoticed. They also knew just how lethal these winged creatures were from the near fatal attack on their father, Duke Redcoat, many weeks ago which had almost cost him his life.

It was Yum who was able to spot the first Buzzard enter into a steep dive as she squeaked an alarm call. Instantly, all four bushy red tails disappeared beneath a convenient clump of Whin bushes and *froze*, perfectly still, so as not to give their presence away. Within five seconds, the most terrifying scream shattered the morning silence on the side of the moor as a wild rabbit met it's *doom* in the claws of the hungry buzzard.

The piercing scream was also a signal to the other members of the buzzard family to join together for an early breakfast of fresh rabbit and Rusty knew only too well that it could so easily have been one, or more, of his immediate family being devoured had not Yum been on full alert.

"OK you lot, they will be fully occupied for a while so lets get cracking" commanded Rusty.

The unusual sight of four rusty red, long tailed, creatures bounding down the open pathway was not an everyday occurrence on the moor, indeed, it was a very rare happening as dozens of docile sheep testified to their presence by lifting up their heads to witness this most unusual happening.

As they moved along at a good pace, Rusty could not help thinking that the invisible force which was propelling them forward, and homeward, in a specific direction, was also the same invisible force which was presenting them with so many life threatening problems. "Whose side are *they* on"? he questioned himself silently, whoever *they* were ?

They all made it safely to the Moor Burn and crossed over the *old railway* sleeper bridge where the path meandered on through difficult terrain with dense whin bushes on either side.

This, Rusty knew, was popular rabbit territory as identified by the large amount of fresh droppings all along the pathway but what concerned him more was the distinct lack of trees. If there was an urgent need to escape from ground level then this would present a major problem so he called an immediate halt in order to survey the land ahead.

As Rusty moved cautiously forward, he suddenly leapt three feet in the air in fearful shock as half a dozen Grey partridge suddenly took flight just in front of him. Their startling cries, plus the sound of their wings clapping, unnerved him so much that his heart was beating three times it's normal speed, such was the impact which caused such an immediate and terrifying reaction.

His leap in the air, however, had given Rusty a brief glimpse of a line of old fence posts, just the job to take a *sneaky deek* at the terrain ahead. Travelling beneath the dense Whin bushes, he soon came upon the first of the posts which, when he quickly scrambled to the top, gave him all the information he needed in an instant.

Scanning the view to the north, Rusty memorised every detail as far as he could see and stored it all in his data base for future reference. The sight which pleased him most was just how much closer they were to the giant stone wall which surrounded the woodland park but the sound, which he now heard from close by, was not so welcome to his ears.

"Yeep, yeep, yeep. Yeep, yeep, yeep" was the repeated alarm call of Blackie Blackbird who, on top of another fence post further to the north, was telling everyone around that danger was lurking in the Whin bushes below.

Other wild birds were nervously flitting and hovering just above the top of the Whins which told Rusty that some evil, sinister, creature was causing havoc not too far away and this warning could not possibly be ignored.

There was no way Rusty could tell just what, or who, the invisible enemy was. It could be a stray domestic Cat, or even a wild one. Maybe a Weasel or a Stoat. Possibly an Adder or maybe a Fox, any of whom would present a very serious risk to his brother, sisters, and himself included, whilst at ground level.

Over to his left the pathway *forked* leaving Rusty with a difficult choice as the four young reds *soldiered* on. To go right would lead them alongside the Moor Burn then on towards the woodland park and, to turn left, the path would take them to the nearby farm house about one hundred yards up on the side of the moor.

Unable to decide immediately which direction to choose, Rusty had to calm his three agitated siblings who also recognised danger nearby. As he glanced to his right, Rusty could see half a dozen black faced sheep, nonchalantly sauntering down the track in single file towards them.

Suddenly, the leading sheep stopped and levelled it's head directly towards a gap in the Whin bushes. A *Pointer dog* could not have performed better.

As it stamped it's foot aggressively to warn the other sheep, his head remained rigid as it stared ahead at the mystery interloper. The indirect warning from the sheep was sufficient to tell Rusty to take the left fork as he squeaked an urgent alarm call to the others and all four *bolted* as fast as their little legs could carry them up towards the farm house.

The unseen interloper turned out to be none other than ferocious Fred Ferret.

Fred had roamed this part of the moor for a long time. He had once been a tame and trained ferret used by a local farmer's son Matthew to catch rabbits. In fact Fred still wore the small leather collar which had been put on by his previous master and very similar to that which Rusty had worn when he was in captivity.

Having escaped his young handler, Fred had enjoyed life in the wild for over a year. It was so much better and there was an ever ready supply of his favourite food as this part of the moor was infested with rabbits.

Being a creamy, beige colour, Fred had to rely mostly on his guile, speed and agility to capture his prey which, on this very day, he did not object to a bit of deadly sport with four young red squirrels.

To-day he thought he'd laid the perfect ambush but did not reckon on the *stupid* sheep from spoiling his plan. Blackie Blackbird's alarm call did not bother Fred, he'd heard it everywhere he travelled on the moor but now it was time to implement plan 'B'.

A ferret is sort of a domesticated weasel, sleek, immensely fast and strong with a streamlined body ideal for squirming down rabbit holes after it's prey.

To-day however, Fred was determined to have a bit of *fun* above ground and what better challenge was there than with a wild, red squirrel. Being four made it even more challenging so how could he lose ?

Ignoring the *stupid* dark faced sheep, Fred doubled back beneath the dense whin bushes with the intention of cutting off the four 'red's' means of escape. What he had not reckoned with however, was the fact that a red squirrel is just about as fast as a ferret, if not faster. Not having ever raced a red squirrel before, Fred was gambling on the *big headed* opinion of his own capability as he simply did not expect to lose this *battle of wits* to-day.

Rusty had, as yet, not identified his enemy but Yum told him breathlessly that, according to Blackie Blackbird's alarm call, the mysterious predator was none other than Fred Ferret. Yum had witnessed a similar experience once before. In fact it was on her very first excursion outside the woodland park in search of hazel nuts. Yum had been fortunate to be up in a tree which gave her a distinct advantage and also a *grandstand* view of Mr Fred Ferret at his everyday, evil, occupation of catching rabbits.

In a flustered gabble, Yum had imparted this knowledge to Rusty with the added advice that, "we must climb up high".

Where the track forked, a direction sign pointed to Herds House Farm as Rusty sped forward along the grass verge with the other three in pursuit. Just around the first bend, the old farm house loomed into view and Rusty knew immediately just which route he was going to take.

With not a single tree nearby, Rusty heeded Yum's advice and stopped right up against the *shoe* of the cast iron down spout which was there for the purpose of discharging rain water from the roof of the house. Quickly he directed the three frantic reds into the down spout with Len leading the way. Once all three were safely inside, Rusty backed into the spout opening, tail first, and placed himself in a defensive position in readiness for the approach of their attacker.

Fred Ferret had seen Rusty just as he had drawn his head inside the spout and made a *bee line* across the farm yard, licking his lips in anticipation of a delicious 'red squirrel' breakfast. He was soon licking his lips but not for the taste of Rusty's blood but, that of his own !

No sooner had Fred Ferret stuck his nose inside the open end of the spout, Rusty, on full alert, attacked with both front paws causing nasty wounds to Fred's *hooter*. Fred had not expected to be caught in that fashion and realised that this red squirrel was smarter than the average red squirrel and, very much smarter than any rabbit. With blood pouring from his wounded nose, Fred was foolish enough to try once more only to be repelled again and his wounds were now twice as bad as before.

'Down spout with shoe outlet at Herds House Farm where the four young Redcoat squirrels sought refuge'

Rusty knew there was no way Fred could dislodge him from the cast iron spout and was sufficiently confident to instruct his three siblings to climb up inside the 'down spout' while he held Fred Ferret at bay. This turned into a bit of a dilemma for Rusty as he could not climb backwards up the spout and still hold Fred Ferret at bay but, at least Milli, Len and Yum were now safe as they peered down at the scene below from their elevated and safe position on the roof above.

The situation between red squirrel and ferret now became a stand off with neither giving way but Rusty held the upper hand or maybe the sharper claws ! There was no way Fred Ferret could dislodge him from the 'down spout' and Fred was also vulnerable outside in the open farm yard.

It didn't take long for the resident watch dog, Ben, to know that something strange was *going on* on his *patch* outside in the yard and barked his disapproval at being unable to get outside to check the matter out.

Mathew, son of the Herds House Farm family, and third in charge, was unable to concentrate on his fiddle music because of the *row* Ben was making, looked from the upstairs window to witness the amazing sight of three red squirrels sitting on the upper spout opposite and Fred Ferret, his one time pet, frantically trying to get into the spout outlet down below.

Intrigued at the scene before him, Matthew dashed quickly downstairs, opened up the *fridge* door and quickly cut a piece of fresh meat from the beef joint, nipped out the back door, into the shed at the rear to get the Larsen trap down from it's hook on the wall.

Deftly, Matthew *primed* the trap with fresh meat and hurried out to the hay shed where he carefully placed the trap between two bales of hay. For the uninitiated, a Larsen Trap is a specially designed cage by a certain Mr Larsen, used to trap Magpies when they create mayhem among the Partridge and Pheasant chicks and other wild birds.

Getting back inside the house, Matthew called Ben and, opening the front door, allowed the dog to bolt forward and streak across the yard at *full pelt* towards the unsuspecting ferret, however, unaccustomed as Ben was at trying to catch a rogue ferret, he could not resist uttering a fit of excitable *yapping* on his approach, thus losing the element of surprise.

In a fraction of a second, Fred Ferret had heeded the early warning and made a sudden dash for the hay shed. Ben however did not attempt to follow Fred Ferret but instead, stuffed his nose into the end of the spout which truly baffled young Matthew.

With his tail going like a *windscreen wiper* on full power, the collie dog was onto something inside the spout which previously Matthew had not realised. He took the dog by the collar and *called him to heel,* With his horn handled stick, Matthew rapped on the cast iron spout a few times when, after a few seconds, out shot a dishevelled red squirrel and scaled the house wall with the greatest of skill and agility to reach his sisters and brother in less than twenty seconds on the spout above.

Matthew had now *sussed* out the scenario in an instant. 'Ferret chases red squirrels who take refuge in the down spout. Ferret thinks he has red squirrel trapped. Collie dog knows something is going on outside and Matthew's action removes the threat to allow the red squirrel to escape'. There now !

Matthew was well satisfied as he returned to his fiddle practise and, for the present, unaware that Fred Ferret was gorging himself on the tastiest piece of meat he'd had since his captive years, oblivious of the fact that there was no escape from his wire mesh Larsen trap situated between two bales of hay !

'*The baited Larson trap all set to capture Fred Ferret*'

From their vantage point up on the eaves of the farm house, all four Redcoat youngsters were relieved that their present torment was over and they were now free to continue on their journey back to meet up with their parents, Duke and Duchess Redcoat, on their home territory in the woodland park and all that lay in store for them on the very last lap of their journey. Or, was it ?

Chapter Twenty

HOME AT LAST

Rusty wasted no time in leading his sisters and brother down off the roof at Herds House Farm from which he had taken final bearings to lead them all safely back to their homeland in the woods near Alnwick

Matthew got just a brief glimpse from his bedroom window of four red squirrels *skedaddling* across the farm yard but was too much absorbed in his music to pay much attention except to think, "I've never seen four red squirrels all together at one time in my life before" !

Picking up the wide track once again, the bright sun spotlighted the four rusty red creatures on the run and transformed their appearance immediately. Their coats positively glistened in the sunlight as they picked up speed, no doubt conscious that they were on the final lap of their journey, especially for Len and Rusty.

Spurred on with this burning desire, Rusty led from the front with all haste, aiming for the high boundary stone wall near to the Recreation Ground and, it was only a matter of a few hundred yards from there to the *finish post* at the East Lodge.

As they paused for a well earned *breather*, Milli advised Rusty to be on the lookout for neighbourhood dogs, out being exercised or else roaming free, as they would undoubtedly present a major problem. One bark from a solitary dog would alarm all the others and all four young Redcoat's lives would really be in peril.

As they cleared the houses on the west side of the town, Rusty steered a different course to skirt around the recreation ground hoping to pick up the boundary wall. This he knew would provide added protection because the high trees of the woodland park were directly on the other side of the wall and would give them a tree top approach to their final destination.

Milli had been *spot on* with her prediction about the threat of domestic dogs.

It only took one curious little 'Yorkie Terrier' to upset Rusty's plan as it sniffed it's way, away from it's owner, to venture over by a clump of Gorse bushes near the boundary wall, no doubt expecting to find an unsuspecting rabbit to have *a bit of a chase* with.

This is exactly what did happen as the little 'Yorkie' flushed out a solitary rabbit who bolted straight into the path of the four travelling red squirrels.

The 'Yorkie's excitable 'yap yap yap' was like a *mobile text message* to all other dogs in the vicinity that a *loose bunny* had been *spooked* and the chase was now on.

Soon the sound of several barking dogs sent fear into the hearts of the four young red squirrels having seen the terrified rabbit streaking over open grassland to escape the chasing pack.

Fortunately for the escaping *bunny*, he made it to the drain hole below the wall and escaped just in the *nick of time* into the woodland park.

Thoughts were flashing back in Rusty's mind about the previous attack on himself and Len by the pack of Fox Hounds way out on the wild moor and how they had just escaped certain death, *by the skin of their teeth*, in a similar fashion.

"Who said lightening never strikes the same way twice", thought Rusty !!!

About six, or more, excited dogs were now in full *gallop* across the Rec', running at an angle towards the boundary wall when they saw their *quarry* disappear below the wall but now their attention was drawn to the four wild red squirrels and their hackles were raised high at the sight of an even better target.

All four young 'reds' were now almost exhausted having travelled at speed for the past half hour and Rusty could now see the high wall looming up before them but, would they all be able to reach it in time ?

Fortune again played it's part as a group of youngsters were enjoying a hectic game of football and now found themselves directly in the path of the chasing dogs. Almost all together, thinking the dogs were about to attack them, they boys challenged the loose pack by shouting, screaming, and waving their arms in the air to ward them off so the dogs were forced to change direction.

This gave the four young red squirrels just a few valuable seconds to make it to the high boundary wall in the 'nick of time' and scramble up on top to safety. They each suffered a broken claw, or two, and bleeding feet however, they were now able to look down at the baying dogs with scorn and relief so much so that Len, in a well timed and traditional red squirrel fashion, *weed* on the yapping dogs below to the absolute joy and delight of his two sisters and brother !

'The long high boundary wall on the south side of the woodland wildlife park, the very last lap of Rusty's return to his homeland. Accompanied by his two sisters Milli and Yum and his brother Len'

At long last, following a weary and most traumatic, dangerous, adventurous, journey, Rusty was quietly overcome with emotion. He knew now that the East Lodge wildlife café was just a short distance away but, what he did not know was that Jack and Matt Jackdaw were just about to announce the fantastic news about the imminent arrival of the four Redcoat youngsters to all present at the East Lodge.

Even as they set off on the very last stretch of their journey home, the heart warming sound of all the wild creatures present at the East Lodge, winged, two and four footed, and whoever else, reached the ears of the *fantastic* four.

The closer they got, at tree top level, the crescendo of whistling, screeching, chirping and squawking woodland voices became almost deafening as the vast crowd of wild life *well wishers* hailed the near arrival of the young Redcoat family, in particular Rusty and his brother Len, who had been missing, presumed lost forever, and who were now only a matter of seconds away from the greatest welcome ever in the whole history of any wildlife community, anywhere on earth !

All four reds could now feel the emotion welling up inside each little body, such was the effect of the electrifying current, excitement and devotion, just a few yards ahead of them that Rusty had to call on every last milligram of self control to warn each of them to be extra careful as they travelled over the tops of the last remaining tall trees. Such was his own loving, passionate, care that he felt for the other young members of his own direct family.

Just below the cheering horde in the trees and on the roof of the East Lodge, down at ground level when the huge cattle truck, which had earlier passed through the woodland park entrance, and trundled towards the exit then slowed to a halt as it parked up at the side of the roadway, just inside the East Lodge entrance.

As the driver climbed down from his cab, he was *dumb struck* at the sound of apparent bedlam and chaos all around the East Lodge. After locking the cab door, as a practice of habit, he then approached the lodge and rapped on the big oak door with it's huge cast iron knocker.

The expectant welcome from the residents of the lodge, Isobel and Oliver, was rather rudely interrupted by the deafening row in the trees above and in the garden surrounding their *fortress* like home so much so that, bemused as they were by all the commotion, their cattle truck driver, and old acquaintance, was quickly ushered inside, away from the messy droppings raining down from the excited flock in the trees above. All the while, despite the *hullaballoo* going on around them, Duke and Duchess Redcoat were mentally recording all that was happening down below as they perched on the very top of a giant Beech tree.

The high pitched squawking of Matt and Jack Jackdaw could be heard above the commotion as they *zoomed* in through the trees as if *jet propelled.* "They're here, they're here" they shouted in order that their news would be noted by all present. This caused the volume of the immediate gathering to increase ten fold as all present screamed their somewhat hysterical, but understandable, welcome to the four youngsters of the noble Redcoat family.

Led by the intrepid Rusty, all four young red squirrels descended from the tree tops on the opposite side of the road and deftly crossed over by way of a flimsy Alder branch, which extended way over the narrow road, almost touching the dense Yew trees at the rear of the East Lodge. They then dropped onto the flat roof of the conveniently parked cattle truck then up into the yew and giant beech trees.

Once in the company of the massive gathering, all four 'reds' were literally *swamped* with love and kindness as every wild creature present wanted to be the first to greet them in the flesh and the melee which resulted was almost like a swarm of bees on a late, hot, autumn day !!!

Red squirrels galore were the strongest and more agile than most present at the *reception party* and were first to join in the emotional welcome for their distant cousins' long awaited return, back to their native homeland in the woodland park.

This mass greeting took place high up on huge, sturdy limbs of several massive beech trees where the large gathering of excited red squirrels met, en masse, to extend their own individual welcome. This inevitably turned out to become one great seething, writhing assembly of squirming red squirrels which, I doubt, nature has ever witnessed before in all it's wildlife history, such was the incredible scene, high up in the monster beech trees at the rear of the East Lodge at the Alnwick woodland wildlife café.

The wily Rusty however had managed to evade much of the joyous invasion and, his eagle eye had already identified the presence of his beloved parents, Duke and Duchess Redcoat, as they now perched much lower, side by side on the outer twigs of a dense Yew tree. In a few well directed leaps and other manoeuvres, Rusty had finally made it to be with his beloved parents once again as he snuggled, rather *sheepishly*, in between them and instantly felt their closeness, warmth and love as they huddled together in a most tender and emotional embrace.

This was not the proper time for making up in *lost red squirrel* talk, words would come later.

This was also an extra special moment to reinstate the close family bond which had been torn apart so long ago and which was to be doubly reinforced as Len appeared on the scene as if by magic. Now all four red squirrels were locked in a tight, silent, embrace, to soak in the enormity of this joyous and emotional reunion, deliriously happy.

Silent now, inasmuch as the noise from the hoard close at hand had drastically reduced in volume, where all present were able to witness the very tender and emotional greeting being shared amongst all six of the, now re-united, Redcoat family who were totally oblivious to all that was going on around them for obvious reasons.

As expected, the red squirrel to red squirrel greetings finally broke up to allow the two, now flustered, Redcoat sisters, Milli and Yum, to share the occasion with the rest of the family and, as if by an act of courtesy, all the visiting reds suddenly calmed down and gathered silently at a respectable distance so they too could witness the home coming celebration of Rusty and his brother Len who were now, at long last, reunited with their natural family.

All the winged and other creatures of the wild woodland who had turned up to partake in the homecoming celebrations of the two lost Redcoat brothers also settled down and, in an almost reverend silence, joined all present in a respectful vigil to say thank you for their safe return.

Duke Redcoat, ever mindful of the importance of this extremely rare occasion, would not let himself be distracted totally from the critical project he had to oversee and quietly excused himself from the rest of his family and beckoned Rusty to follow him inside the dense foliage of the Yew tree. Rusty felt the overwhelming feeling of joy drain from him as his father explained, in precise detail, the devastating news about the deadly virus which was now present in their ancient family woodland habitat and further explained to his son the very nature of his plan to evacuate all red squirrels from around the Alnwick area to far up north into Scotland where they would, hopefully, be rid of the *deadly scourge* forever.

Rusty soon recovered his composure and sheer pride as his wise old father took over. He wondered at the bravery of this natural leader and the task he had taken on filled him also with a sense of direct responsibility for all his indigenous, red coated, squirrel family of direct and distant relatives, plus any others, who had gathered at the command of his father Duke.

Rusty had been asked by his father to assemble the whole gathering of red squirrels in the ancient beech trees at the back yard of the East Lodge. Whilst he was in the process of rounding up all the 'red' community, especially the wayward, playful youngsters, something rather familiar caught his eye. It was the markings on the side of the huge cattle lorry parked down below.

It was the deep seated memory of something he had seen on the magic box in Sonny's bedroom long ago when he was in captivity far away which aroused his curiosity but he pushed it from his mind to concentrate on the immediate task in hand.

Once all the red squirrels were assembled, Duke took over to lecture the gathering on the details of his plan as well as to explain the desperate need for a speedy departure from their natural homeland for everyone's sake. Gasps of astonishment could be heard all around as Duke completed his lecture as the bewildered assembly tried to take in the severity of what they had just learned.

Nevertheless, all present, apart from some of the wayward youngsters, had eaten well all day as instructed by Duke Redcoat and all were in remarkably good physical condition in readiness for the long, planned, journey which lay before them. Duke's final words to all present were that, "they must all stay close together here at the woodland, wildlife café and to get a good sleep once the sun went down in readiness for their historic journey up north to Scotland at first light in the morning".

Content that all that could be done had been done, Rusty enjoyed the deep friendly greetings extended to him personally by so many of his blood line. Many complete strangers from far afield likewise greeted him, and almost all, wanted him to tell them about his adventures in captivity and his ultimate escape and return journey.

Rusty assured everyone they would all be told about his experiences, all in good time, once they had arrived safely north of the border.

The nagging doubt in Rusty's mind about the strange cattle lorry parked below would just not go away, and this troubled him sorely. As nothing would materialise inside his tired head he sought out his mother Duchess for comfort intending to spend the rest of their last afternoon together in their woodland home.

Soon they were chatting away about this and that when Duchess surprisingly asked her son, "Even though you are finally back home Rusty, please tell me what is troubling you" ? Rusty was really taken aback at the powerful instincts of his mother whom he had not seen since he was a tiny kitten so long ago.

"It's only a *niggling* doubt Mother. There is something about that cattle lorry parked below which intrigues me and my tired brain will not tell me what it is".

Duchess Redcoat went on to tell Rusty that it was her belief that the driver of the cattle truck, which had, incidentally, entered the woodland park earlier in the day with a consignment of Highland cattle, probably for the West Farm, is not a local man. The driver, Duchess continued, is definitely a friend of Oliver and Isobel who reside in the East Lodge and, she said, "As I speak, he is now with them in the Lodge, no doubt having some well earned refreshment, and a good '*blether*' before returning home".

"By the way. He also speaks with the same Scottish *tongue* as Oliver and Isobel and that, maybe, is the friendly connection," said Duchess.

His mother's words were the very key which unlocked Rusty's *memory bank.* "That's it mother, highland cattle, from Scotland. Shhhhhhh" he said quietly to her as he put a front paw to his lips then quickly descended to ground level to examine the huge cattle truck in more detail.

One particular word in clear big letters on the side panel said S C O T L A N D, for that is how Rusty recalled the same name he had seen for himself on Sonny's *magic box* so long ago.

The vision which was now so vivid in Rusty's mind was of a moving picture he had seen on the *magic box* in Sonny's bedroom when in captivity. This story showed the rusty red, shaggy Highland cattle which are the native cattle of Scotland. "That's it" he almost screamed out loud and he now knew in an instant that he must go to his father Duke without delay.

Chapter Twenty One

THE FINAL DEPARTURE

'The lorry which made a timely visit to the woodland wildlife park.'

Having taken in every important detail of the lorry parked down below, Rusty sped upwards into the trees to find his father Duke who was just about to explain in detail to every red squirrel present, elaborate details of the proposed march to Scotland at first light to-morrow.

Not wanting to frighten them off with facts about hardship, hunger, danger, tiredness and fatigue, plus a host of other hazards, Duke intended to choose his words carefully and to instruct all present of the need to obey his precise instructions so as to progress as a team to their final destination.

Duke's train of thought was suddenly interrupted as Rusty appeared close by him in a most determined and serious manner.

As father and son Redcoat were deep in conversation, Duke's ever watchful eye told him, subconsciously, that the afternoon sun was rapidly dropping over the high ground to the west.

As he listened to what Rusty had to tell him about the big cattle truck down below, and all that it entailed with regard to a possible means of escape for all concerned, Duke Redcoat reflected immediately on the words which wise old 'Orny' the Tawny Owl had spoken to him earlier in the day when he said "Look for the clue which will be your saviour in all this trauma" or words to that effect, and now Duke had to accept that he had failed to recognise that vital clue.

Fortunately for all concerned, the smart young Rusty Redcoat had the wisdom to have recognised the significance of the big cattle truck and the key to the success of his father's plan to evacuate all the red squirrel community safely away from the disease ridden woodlands around Alnwick and this very fact had just been explained to Duke.

'The key which unlocked the secret', and cunning advice which 'Orny' had passed on to him, caused Duke Redcoat to be beside himself with relief, pride and admiration, together with the total acceptance and understanding of the brilliant plan his clever son Rusty had devised. This was more than he could ever have believed possible.

"We must not waste a moment" Duke told Rusty. "Soon it will be dark and the driver could leave at any time".

Hastily, Duke passed on a message to the more senior members of the local red squirrel community that they all must do exactly as young Rusty tells them without question or delay.

Rusty had now discovered that the overhanging Yew branches stretched right out and were, in fact, touching the near side of the big cattle truck. This stroke of good fortune would allow easy access into the truck through the narrow gaps in the side panels.

Rusty could now clearly see inside which had been cleaned out and a fresh bed of straw strewn over the floor. Even better still, Rusty was delighted to see half a dozen large bales of straw stacked up inside the body of the vehicle which he knew instantly would add significantly to the comfort of the travelling 'passengers'.

Off he sped into the trees and quickly told several of the more senior reds just what they had to do and they obeyed in an instant. Soon, scores of excited red squirrels were scrambling through the narrow gaps to get inside the cattle truck where the elders commanded total silence and order.

Rusty found it impossible to keep an accurate count as the Yew tree was heaving with a frenzy of excited activity. They all, finally, got themselves safely inside the truck and were instructed to hide beneath the straw, at least until the truck got underway.

The old Chief of the Red Squirrel Clan was now busy patrolling all the trees nearby searching for any stragglers as, he had decided, he deserved the right to be the very last red squirrel to get into the truck in fact, be the very last to leave their ancient, woodland, habitat in Alnwick, which had been the wonderful home of the Redcoat dynasty for many hundreds of years.

Rusty likewise was making a last minute check and was satisfied that he was able to account for all the members of his own beloved family being present inside the cattle truck, except for his father of course.

Rusty also recognised the absolute, emotional, pain his father Duke was going through at this precise moment but was more than a little anxious that he had not yet entered the wagon. He was also smart enough to understand the innermost feelings of both his parents who were being forced to evacuate their ancestral homelands in order to save the whole local red squirrel population from a certain agonising death by the lethal virus which the invading Grey squirrel was transmitting to the Red squirrel population.

The whole of Duke's life had been spent in this woodland park, as with his forefathers, so the wrench of having to leave was just too terrible to even imagine. Yet, Rusty was confident that his father would come on board in his own time once he had bid his silent goodbye to all that had been so truly dear and wonderful for him in so many ways throughout his long, illustrious, life.

. Darkness had now descended outside and Rusty was thoroughly pleased at the way in which all the red squirrel contingent had settled down inside the lorry. Squeaks of excitement could be heard from beneath the straw from the youngsters who were treating the whole episode as a great adventure but there was no mistaking the sniffles and muffled sobs of several adults who could not control their emotions as tears of sorrow could not be held in check at the sadness of it all.

Suddenly, rays of artificial light beamed through the gaps in the side of the truck as the outside lights of the East Lodge illuminated the rear of the premises.

This instantly silenced all the stowaways hidden inside the truck as Rusty detected the sound of the heavy latch being lifted on the entrance door of the lodge as it opened into the gloomy darkness of the evening.

This increased the floodlit scene even greater and human voices could clearly be heard close by the huge vehicle. Rusty easily detected the friendly tone of the voices, all with a similar accent and soon, footsteps were now audible as the driver made a complete circuit of his vehicle, no doubt as a regular check, before moving off.

The atmosphere inside the lorry was now so tense that Rusty fully expected that maybe one, or even more, of the 'illegal' red squirrel occupants would make some attempt to escape but, to his delight, and relief, not a single movement could be detected from anyone.

Human calls of "Goodbye, Safe journey, Call again" could clearly be heard outside as the driver opened his cab door and climbed aboard. "Cheerio" was his reply.

The sudden vibration which shook the whole vehicle when the engine was switched on caused panic among most of the *passengers*. Many shot up from beneath the straw covering to seek safety on top of the bales thinking they would suffer terrible injuries if they stayed on the hard floor.

As the engine revved up slightly the truck moved gently backwards and, after a deafening blast on the horn, moved slowly forward on to the road way. It was at this very late stage in the proceedings when Rusty noticed his father Duke clambering in through the gap just in the nick of time as the big truck manoeuvred it's way gently through the archway then picked up speed, down towards the main road into the darkened gloom of the night, hopefully, on it's long journey north to Scotland.

The presence of Duke Redcoat seemed to have a sobering and relaxing effect on all present, such was the respect the red squirrel community had for their leader.

Duke wanted all present to know that all was well but, because of the loud drone of the huge engine, was unable to make his voice heard. After about ten minutes, the whole of the interior was suddenly lit up as the driver steered the truck into the nearby service station to fill up with fuel for the long journey ahead.

When all was quiet, as the big engine was switched off, Duke took the opportunity to address all present to tell them that everything was going to plan and that they were now on their way to begin a new life in Scotland .

He then surprised his audience when he announced that it was young Rusty Redcoat they had to thank for this miraculous idea to escape, which had saved each and every one of them from the long, perilous and torturous journey to Scotland on foot as Duke Redcoat had originally planned, and that it was young Rusty's smart thinking to take advantage of a late development by 'borrowing' the giant truck, so to speak !

Duke was blunt, direct, and honest when he went on to tell them that many of those present would not have survived the long journey on foot as a lot would surely have died on the long trek north. As it was, this wonderful and surprising mode of travel would ensure that all present would arrive in Scotland safely.

Finally, Duke caused further gasps of amazement when he announced that, from this very moment, he was retiring from his leadership role of the Redcoat family with the Alnwick Red Squirrel contingent because he was now too old and so terribly upset to be leaving his beloved homeland. Now he was relinquishing all duties by handing over all his official authority and responsibilities to his young son Rusty.

Duke, with Duchess Redcoat proudly by his side, requested all present to give Rusty the same loyalty and devotion they had always shown towards himself and that, from now on, Rusty was to be their new leader.

As if on cue, the big engine sprang to life and off they sped into the darkness of the motorway to where ever they were about to be taken !!

Rusty soon took up his position beside his parents, along with Milli, Len and Yum., so proud indeed of his new role as leader of this travelling band of desperate Red squirrels, desperate to find a new, safe, life in Scotland away from the deadly Grey squirrel pox virus which would so easily have wiped them all out.

All was seemingly loving and content when suddenly Len whispered to no one in particular, "What will happen if this cattle wagon is not going to Scotland" ?????

With gasps of surprise the Redcoat Family looked at one another, seeking an answer to the not so stupid question Len had put forward. Duchess supported Len somewhat when she ventured to add that no one knew for sure that the cattle truck 'was' going to Scotland and, in fact, she stated that, "For all we know, we could well be heading to the far south of England, and what then" ?

This was indeed the first challenge of Rusty's leadership and his wisdom was certainly, and rightfully, being called into question.

"It is all a matter of logic and reasoning" he boldly uttered. "there were just too many coincidences to be ignored and besides, did not 'Orny' the wise old Tawny Owl advise father to be watchful for the vital clue which would provide the very means of our escape." Rusty continued, "All I did was to carefully analyse all that was being presented to me and I simply trusted in my own reasoning to come to the conclusion that this just had to be".

To qualify and quantify his statement, Rusty was quick to point out

"Since we left the service station, we have been travelling steadily northwards towards the Scottish Border"!

Len stuttered a quick apology, " I'm sorry, but I only wanted to be sure we were definitely going to Scotland" to which Rusty replied:- "You should know me well enough by now dear brother that I am fully confident but, your question was perfectly justified."

With that authoritative remark from the new Redcoat leader, they all settled down to form a comfortable bed on the bales of straw, just as all the other 'rusty red' travellers had already done and they were soon comfortably settled down for whatever length of time it would take to arrive at their final destination.

The steady motion of the huge cattle truck, plus the rhythmic hum of the engine, eventually had all the bushy red tailed passengers sleeping peacefully as they journeyed mile after mile northwards towards their new safe haven.

Some were covered in the warm straw, others, especially the adults, used their bushy red tail in the customary fashion as a duvet but all were 'sound as tops' after what had been the most eventful, exciting and exhausting day of their whole lives.

After a while, anyone who would have looked inside the big cattle truck would not have seen a solitary red squirrel for all had now buried themselves well beneath the straw to keep out the bitter cold of the night air as the wind whistled and rushed inside the body of the truck through the side panels as it trundled along the Border roads.

Not even the odd flash of light from passing vehicles disturbed the sleeping 'passengers' who, for them in particular, it was just as if they were asleep in the tree tops on a windy night !

Rusty must have been the only one who had not 'switched off' altogether. His mind was too active because of the responsibility resting on his young shoulders yet, even as he dozed fitfully, he was extremely confident and alert just in case something should go wrong.

Chapter Twenty Two

'THE END OF THE BEGINNING' !!

The truck stopped briefly a couple of times at traffic lights and road works when Rusty strained his eyes to see if he could identify anything through the slot in the side of the lorry but little was visible in the darkness of the night. Only the bright headlights of the truck lit up the road way ahead as they journeyed on, and on, and on.

What seemed to Rusty to be an eternity, little doubts did actually penetrate his mind as to where they really were but, brief glimpses, now and then, of the half moon in the night sky convinced him that all was going to plan and that they were now heading north west.

At one stage in the journey Rusty almost squealed with delight as a large sign on the road side came into view. The big, bold, letters were so clearly visible which Rusty was able to recognise as SCOTLAND WELCOMES YOU.

'This road sign was positive proof for Rusty to know that they were now in Scotland'

'The sign post which proved the truck full of stowaway Red Squirrels had finally arrived at their final destination'

Further on at one stop for some road works, the beam of the enormous headlights lit up the roadway ahead. Rusty was squinting out through the gap in the panelling and, as the traffic lights changed to green, the truck moved up through the gears when the headlights picked out yet another road sign which displayed, in big black letters, the word GORDON. Rusty's computer like memory reflected on his days in captivity when he had seen something on Sonny's magic box in the bedroom about 'Gordon Highlanders' who were the brave soldiers from Scotland.

This, at last, was positive proof for him that they had definitely made it to Gordon in Scotland.

Rusty's eyes soon became accustomed to the gloom inside the truck as he could just make out the main framework from the inside and, moreover, pairs of little sparkling lights reflecting in the gloom each time an advancing vehicle passed by. These were reflections in the eyes of the adult members of the 'redcoat brigade' who had awakened from their slumbers and were naturally curious as to what was happening.

Rusty, now perched proudly on top of the highest bale, took the chance each time a passing vehicle lit up the inside of the truck to give an assuring wave to those watching inside.

He could not of course give a 'thumbs up' sign simply because Red Squirrels do not have thumbs, they only have four fingers on each of their forepaws but five toes on each foot.

Finally the truck came to a permanent halt. After a bit of manoeuvring, the engine was switched off. Then a 'clang' as the driver shut the door of his cab, followed by the sound of footsteps on a gravel surface when another door opened and closed then all was so very still and quiet indeed.

"All of you try to go back to sleep" Rusty's voice echoed quietly in the body of the truck. "I think we have arrived safely but you will all need as much rest as possible for, at first light, I will see if there is any water to quench our thirst."

All fell silent, now that Rusty had assured them of their safe arrival and so, with a contented mind, sleep came easily to the travel weary band of red squirrels.

Rusty dozed for a while and dreamt of 'Orny' the Tawny Owl who hooted in the woods to advertise his presence. It was always a comforting sound to all red squirrels because 'Orny' acted as a watchman and would raise the alarm in case of any danger.

Alarmingly, Rusty realised he was not dreaming at all. Orny's soft call was not actually in his dream at all and suddenly old Duke Redcoat made a rather sleepy eyed appearance to take up a position beside Rusty.

"Well done my son, I am so very, very proud of you" he said quietly "but you have not yet got the many, long, years' experience behind you to recognise all the woodland sounds and signals. What wise old 'Orny' is telling you is that all is well and that he flew all the way up here in advance to warn your uncle, my cousin, Big Bob Blacktail, to be prepared to meet up with us all at first light."

As the morning light intensity increased, so did the activity inside the truck as a great many little red heads began to appear above the straw. Rusty recognised thirst and hunger in each pair of eyes which did not trouble him unduly just yet. What did please him most of all was that, not one pair of eyes showed any fear whatsoever.

Rusty could feel the excitement building as the good news was being broadcast to all present.

Old Duke continued to relay the rest of 'Orny's' message in that, ' we must all take a good drink once we leave the truck then feast on a breakfast of corn and dried beans from the corn shed at the rear of the truck. We will all have to be absolutely quiet for fear of alarming the resident dogs'.

As dawn light slowly emerged, Rusty alighted from the truck, his first ever time on Scottish soil. Satisfied that all seemed OK, he climbed back inside then delegated his brother Len to check out the farm for any resident dogs, big or small, and to report back.

Next he called on his two excited sisters, Milli and Yum, and gave them the task of locating the corn shed. Rusty did not want red squirrels swarming all over this strange place and off the girls went, tails swishing with pride having been given an important task from their now 'illustrious' brother.

Len soon reported back to inform Rusty that he could not detect any dogs outside in the farm yard and added that there was a small stream at the rear of the farm where all would be able to quench their thirst. Next through the gap leapt his two breathless sisters who arrived with news that the corn shed was close by and the door was slightly ajar so getting inside would not present a problem.

Rusty called for attention from all present and explained the situation. Milli and Yum would lead the way to the corn shed and all would follow in an orderly fashion. Rusty emphasised that total silence was to be observed until they were well away from the farm and, with that, Milli and Yum led the whole procession towards the corn shed for their first ever Scottish breakfast !

Rusty and his father Duke were last to leave the truck with Rusty having a quiet chuckle to himself at the thought of the driver's surprised reaction when he would look inside his truck to see the absolute mess of loose straw !!

The feeding frenzy inside the corn shed was a sight to behold. Anyone would think they'd not eaten for five whole days as the small army of red squirrels feasted, somewhat rarely, on lovely fresh wheat and tasty broad beans.

It did not take long for each to take their fill and Rusty again directed everyone to move out to the stream to slake their thirst as out they all trooped along like a squad of well trained soldiers. Duke and Duchess simply looked on in awe.

Having made a final check, as with the inside of the cattle truck, the corn shed looked as if a herd of cattle had been in there as Rusty made for the door opening. He did not like creating such havoc but how can anyone control three score plus of starving red squirrels?

His sixth sense, yet again, prompted him to pause just as he was about to leave the corn shed and his gaze was mysteriously directed up to the rafters above and there, in the early morning gloom, sat no one other than 'Orny' the Tawny Owl.

Rusty at first stared in astonishment then, remembering his father's praises of such a wise old owl, lifted his right paw and saluted the very creature who had the extraordinary foresight to have predicted the most unusual means of escape for the whole red squirrel community from the Alnwick woodlands only a matter of a few hours ago.

As with 'Orny's last meeting with Duke, the old wise owl acknowledged Rusty's salute with a brief 'hoot' then suddenly he swooped silently down and finally up through the air vent opening in the gable end and disappeared into the early morning sky.

The crucial time of the whole exercise was now about to take place which was to seek immediate refuge in the nearby woods without delay.

Rusty soon took up his rightful place at the head of the column of red squirrels and, taking a bearing from the early morning sun, set off at a slow trot north westward in the direction of a vast area of woodland with a long trail of excited red squirrels in convoy behind.

Keeping close to a large hawthorn hedge, Rusty set a steady pace to get them all clear of the farm buildings as the sun climbed higher in the Scottish sky.

The whole troupe consisted of young and old alike and Rusty was conscious of the disabilities of some of the elder members, his own parents included, and soon called a halt when he felt they were now a safe distance away from the farm.

Eyeing a solitary old oak tree in the hedgerow up ahead, Rusty left instructions for all to take a brief rest then, invited his father Duke to join him as he sped forward towards the old oak tree.

Pausing to allow his elderly dad to catch up, Rusty's attention was drawn to movement up ahead in another nearby oak tree. This movement was from none other than his father's Scottish cousin, Big Bob Blacktail and his family, waiting to greet the new comers, whose swishing tail was signalling a welcome to his Redcoat relatives in the traditional fashion.

Rusty beckoned to the new contingent to come forward and very soon tails were swishing all over the place as the two parties raced to greet each other, The hawthorn hedge was soon alive with a heaving mass of red coated, bushy tailed squirrels where their fur coats sparkled in the bright morning sunlight.

Duke Redcoat and Big Bob Blacktail did their best to introduce each other's family members but the youngsters were all too eager to show off their acrobatic skills to one another as the hedgerow was a seething horde of wild and energetic activity.

Rusty, in his wisdom, stayed just far enough away from the hectic activity so as to take in the nature of their new surroundings. The wood land ahead looked extremely healthy with a good mix of beech and pine trees plus an abundance of hazels on the outer perimeter and he was anxious to get all his new found family away from open ground and into the secure cover of the trees.

How could he break up this fantastic gathering which he knew, full well, to be a most remarkable feat of nature which had probably never, ever, occurred before in Red Squirrel history on such a large scale. Having got them all here safe and sound, he would consider it extremely irresponsible of himself if only one of his 'flock' should be taken by an unseen predator, hence he was anxious to continue the march to the safety of the woodland.

Having been introduced to most of the Blacktail family, Rusty could not help notice that there was absolutely no difference in the way the two red squirrel families, from both sides of the border, communicated in red squirrel language which prompted him to realise just what a strange bunch these humans really are !!!

Rusty also soon realised just who had been responsible for carrying the valuable advance news from Alnwick's woodland park up into Scotland and the Blacktail family. It had to be the wise old '*Orny*' the Tawny Owl of course and Rusty knew he would forever be indebted to this remarkable creature for all he had done to help the red squirrels of the Alnwick Redcoat Clan during their recent plight.

As natural as any born leader would react, Rusty signalled his intention to move on and, without the slightest objection, from either family or friends, they at once moved forward on what was to be the final and absolute last leg of their miraculous journey to safety.

Smart as Rusty Redcoat was, and he really, really, was very smart for such a youngster, he firmly believed they had got so far from the farm on their way to their new habitat without being observed but, he had not reckoned on a young, and equally smart, apprentice gamekeeper called Cameron who was stationed in a cleverly concealed 'hide', and, who had just witnessed the whole amazing scene with total incredulity.

Realising he had been witness to one of nature's greatest ever phenomenon, even of their earlier arrival at the farm in the old cattle truck, which he had witnessed through his binoculars, Cameron silently vowed to himself that he would tell everyone about this wonderful and remarkable rusty red creature for, what he had just seen was beyond his comprehension yet, he knew in his very bones that this was one of nature's finest miracles.

Not knowing they were being observed by young Cameron, Rusty led the procession the last few metres from the hawthorn hedge and through the wire strand fencing into their new abode in the vast, ever welcoming, Scottish woodland.

The woodland floor was strewn with large quantities of beech mast, the fruit of the beech tree, and pine cones galore when, once he was sure that the very last straggler had climbed through the fence, Rusty sought a convenient perch, half way up an old Scots pine, and with his heart bursting with pride, he let out a huge sigh of relief. One day, perhaps it may just be the dreadful squirrel disease in England will be eradicated and again, maybe, some of the English Redcoat breed will be able to safely return south of the border to there native woodlands in and around Alnwick. Who knows ?

Rusty was now totally proud, happy, and content, to be safely with his own family at long last and now, entirely satisfied, Rusty Redcoat thought of the wonderful new life which lay ahead for his beloved Redcoat family, and all their new Scottish rusty red friends and relatives, which they would enjoy in their new and safe surroundings in Scotland and, thoroughly exhausted, promptly fell into a sound and well earned, peaceful, sleep.

THE END

ACKNOWLEDGMENTS

I wish to thank those listed below for their kindness and help, in whatever way, throughout the preparation and publication of Volume Two of 'The Adventures of Rusty Redcoat', without which, I very much doubt if the book would ever have been completed satisfactorily, if at all :-

Professor David & Rosemary Bellamy, Maureen Macgregor, Callum Macgregor, Joe Vickers, Kevan McKeag, Isobel & *Oliver* Grant, Rose & *Chris* Mossman, Matthew Jordan, Jack and Matt Robson, Colin Graham, Hazel & Jim Cochrane with son Cameron, Bill King, Colin Heathcote and, last but not least, Azure Printing.
NB:- Starred names indicate the late Oliver and Chris.

The Real Rusty Redcoat